PRAISE FOR
THE TEMPTATION SAGA

"Is it hot in here? Congratulations, Ms. Hardt. You dropped me into the middle of a scorching hot story and let me burn."
~ Seriously Reviewed

"I took this book to bed with me and I didn't sleep until 4 a.m. Yes, it's that damn engrossing, so grab your copy now!"
~Whirlwind Books

"Temptation never tasted so sweet... Both tempting, and a treasure... this book held many of the seductive vices I've come to expect from Ms. Hardt's work."
~Bare Naked Words

Taming

ANGELINA

THE TEMPTATION SAGA
BOOK FOUR

WATERHOUSE PRESS

Taming

ANGELINA

THE TEMPTATION SAGA
BOOK FOUR

This one is for Celina Summers—thank you for your belief in me and my work. You're the best!

CHAPTER ONE

Long black lashes fringed eyes like perfect emeralds. Cheeks shimmered the color of the palest pink rose. Dark hair hung in two ponytails on either side of an oval face. The red-and-white gingham blouse tied below round breasts—with just a touch of cleavage showing—screamed country girl. The Daisy Dukes, long shapely legs, and fire-engine red toenails peeking out from strappy leather flip-flops screamed siren.

Tall, too. He loved tall women. At six-three, he liked his women to fit his frame.

His groin tightened. He'd never been immune to a pretty woman, and she was about as gorgeous as he'd seen—the perfect combination of innocence and heat, sparkle and sultry, virtue and corruption. How would those cherry lips feels against his own? Against...other places?

The two ponytails that would be ridiculous on most women worked on her. Dark curls tumbled over each shoulder. He imagined her sans blouse, sans hair ribbons, that silky hair cascading over peachy-pink shoulders, rosy-tipped breasts.

How it might feel between his fingers, brushing his chest...

Good lord, she is beautiful.

Then she spoke.

"Hand, I'm looking for Rafe Grayhawk."

Hand? Not so beautiful inside. The derision in her tone was unmistakable. He fought the urge to ignore her. He was an employee here at McCray Landing. If this woman was looking for him, she probably had a reason.

"I'm Rafe Grayhawk."

She whipped her hands to her round hips. "I hear you can teach me to ride."

Huh? Who is this woman anyway? She vaguely resembled his boss's wife, though Catie was more refreshing, less "nose-stuck-in-the-air."

"I can teach anyone to ride, honey." He eyed her up and down. "But not in that getup. Who are you, anyway?"

"Angelina Bay. Catie's sister. And don't call me honey."

Rafe held out his hand. "Nice to meet you."

She didn't return the gesture. He dropped his hand back to his side.

"I used to ride a little. I was rodeo queen quite a while ago. But I didn't keep up with it. My daddy says if I'm going to own one of his ranches someday it's high time I learned to ride decently. We don't have any hands at our ranch who have the time or talent to teach me, in his opinion. Daddy wants the best. According to Chad McCray, you're it."

"Why not ask your sister? She's as good a rider as anyone."

"Clearly you haven't heard the good news." Angelina scuffed one sandaled foot in the dirt of the stall. "She's expecting, and since she had a miscarriage the first time, she and Chad are being ridiculously overprotective this time."

Didn't sound unreasonable to Rafe. His mother had struggled with miscarriages and his father had been very protective, but Angelina's voice registered indignation over her sister's decision to put her pregnancy first.

Teach this piece of work to ride? Not in this lifetime.

He turned back to the horse he was currying. "I'm afraid I can't help you. McCray expects all his hands to put in forty hours a week here."

"I already okayed it through him. Didn't I just say he said you're the best to teach me? Sheesh."

Eye roll. He wasn't looking at her, but he knew her pupils were curving upward against her lids.

"Darlin', you've got a sight to learn about askin' for a favor."

"I'm not asking for a favor, hand. You'll be well paid."

Hand again? Christ, I have a name. He turned and gazed into those eyes clear as the Mediterranean Sea. "Well paid, huh? Just how much constitutes 'well paid' to you?"

"Fifty dollars an hour."

A fair price, for sure. Not worth it to put up with this prima donna, though.

"Make it a hundred."

The porcelain hands dashed to her hips again.

"A hundred? Are you kidding me? Fifty is the going rate around here."

"Then I'm sure you won't have any problem finding someone else at that price. Nice meeting you." He turned his back to her.

"But Chad says you're the best."

"The man speaks the truth." Rafe smoothed the gelding's dark mane.

"Seventy-five is as high as I'll go."

Rafe pursed his lips. Seventy-five dollars an hour would go a long way helping his father get out of that damned trailer park. For the last couple of years, Rafe and his brother, Tom, had been putting all their extra money toward a place in Arizona for Jack Grayhawk. Since the death of Rafe's mother, his dad had been wasting away in that old dump. Though only fifty, he'd had to leave construction work after a debilitating injury to his hip. He could still get around, but work was out of the question. He drew a small disability pension, but it wasn't enough. He also suffered from chronic asthma, and though Colorado weather wasn't bad, the dryer Arizona weather and mild winters would be better. Yeah, this money would sure help. Rafe turned around and gazed at the slender woman. Spending time looking at Angelina Bay would be no hardship. Still, to put up with her attitude...

"The price is a hundred. Take it or leave it."

"I'll leave it."

The beauty turned on her heels and marched toward the door of the barn.

Shit, I should have taken the seventy-five.

He could have made life easier for his dad. Jack could take Lilia, the Mexican woman who'd kept house for him for the last five years, with him. Since Finola Grayhawk had passed on three years ago, Lilia cooked and cleaned in exchange for room and board in Rafe and Tom's old room. Lilia had reduced her hours as a receptionist to part time to help keep house for Jack. The two would have had a wonderful new life in Arizona.

Ah well, Rafe had no doubt saved himself a lifetime's worth of headache. He put the currycomb down and grabbed the stiff bristle brush. This particular gelding, Adonis, loved the stiff bristle brush. Rafe started at the neck with short flicking motions. "That's a good boy."

A throat cleared behind him. He turned. Angelina.

"You still here? Thought you'd marched out in a huff."

"A hundred it is then, hand."

"There ain't enough money in the world for me to put up with you calling me 'hand.'"

"That's what I call all the hands."

"They have names, you know."

"You expect me to remember all those names?"

"Why not? They remember yours, don't they?"

"That's different. I'm the boss's daughter, and there's only one of me."

Thank God. If another Angelina existed, he'd lose all hope for the world. "You're not the boss's daughter here."

"I'm the boss's sister-in-law."

"Whatever. You want my help? The price is a hundred an hour, and if you call me 'hand' one more time, all deals are off."

"Fine. Rafe, then."

"How about Mr. Grayhawk?"

"You can't be serious."

"Oh, I am, Miss Bay." *Let's see how she handles this one.*

"Of course you should call me Miss Bay. I'm the boss and you're the help."

Help? Seriously? Normally he'd think twice about getting into it with his boss's sister-in-law, but Chad McCray respected him and his work, and this little snot brought out the worst in him. "I obviously have something you want. I won't deal with disrespect from anyone, especially not a flouncy ranch girl."

Hands to hips again. Did she have two indentations there? "Girl? I happen to be thirty-two years old."

Thirty-two? He'd have guessed her younger than his own age of twenty-five. The years had been kind to Miss Bay. She had the skin and body of a nineteen-year-old. She was a beauty. On the outside, at least.

"Thirty-two years old and acting like a spoiled brat? Grow up, Angelina."

"Miss Bay."

"Angelina. And you'll call me Rafe. I hate Mr. Grayhawk."

She tapped her foot on the barn floor. "It was your idea."

"I was trying to make a point. You were being disrespectful."

"I'm not used to being respectful to hands."

"Well, get used to it. We're people, just like you, and disrespect hurts us, just like it hurts you." Though he doubted she'd ever experienced disrespect.

Her eyes widened—just a little, but he'd made her think. For a second, anyway.

"All right...*Rafe*. When can we start?"

"You got a horse?"

"Yes. Just bought her. A beautiful black mare named Belle."

"Have her brought over by seven tonight."

"Okay."

"And I'll see you tomorrow. Six a.m. sharp."

This time when her hands flew to her hips her eyes turned to saucers. "Six a.m.? Sorry. I don't do the crack of dawn."

Rafe shook his head. "And you expect to own your father's ranch someday? Do you have any idea what time he gets up? Chad and Catie are up before five every morning."

"I'm not Catie."

She was right about that. Did the two of them really come from the same gene pool? The physical evidence was there, but little else.

"Six a.m.," he said, "and wear clothes suitable for riding."

She stormed out, sulking.

Rafe chuckled. No way would she show up.

★ ★ ★

"Angie, how are you?" Debra Montgomery took her arm. "What can we show you today?"

"Whatever you have that's new."

Deb nodded. "I'll call in the reserves."

Angie was known around town for her shopping sprees. She ignored the snotty remarks that she alone kept Deb's Boutique in business. Right now she wanted new clothes, and then she'd head over to the beauty shop for some pampering.

Because she felt like it, that's why.

"We just got in some great new studded jeans from New York," Deb said. "I'll have Lori bring some out in your size."

Angie tried on six pairs of jeans, discarded three, and added the other three to her pile. "I'll need some shirts to go with these," she told Lori, the red-haired clerk she hadn't seen before.

Lori brought in shirt after shirt, but none suited Angie. She piled them back into Lori's arms. "Don't you have anything that doesn't look like it came from a discount store tent sale? Sheesh!"

Lori sighed. "I'll check with Deb."

Deb herself came over. "I'm sorry our selection of blouses isn't to your liking today, Angie. You know I stock only the latest fashions."

Angie rolled her eyes. "Do you have anything else?"

"Lori's getting a few more for you."

"Maybe you should light a fire under her. Your new clerk is incredibly slow."

Deb smiled. Deb always smiled. She had to. Angie spent a lot of money in her boutique.

Lori came out with four more blouses. Angie touched the fabric. "Is this supposed to be silk?"

"That one's rayon," Lori said.

"Rayon? A man-made fabric?"

"Rayon is a semi-synthetic, actually," Deb said. "All the top houses in New York and Europe use it. You know that."

"Whatever." Angie took the blouses. "I'll try them on." She walked back into the dressing room.

"How do you stand her?" she heard Lori whisper.

Angie shook her head as her temper rose. "You may want to tell your new clerk to install soundproof doors on your dressing rooms. I heard that!"

"I'm sorry, Angie," Deb's voice said. "I'll take care of you myself today."

Angie discarded three of the blouses into Deb's waiting arms. "You should fire that new girl. Hasn't she ever heard that the customer is always right?"

"Lori knows fashion," Deb said. "I'm sorry she insulted you, but I won't fire her. She came highly recommended, and just in the week she's been here she's made more sales than Gwen did all month."

"Fine," Angie said. "Put the clothes on my tab and have them delivered. And don't expect to see me in here again as long as that little snot is working here."

She walked out the door and headed to Judy's Beauty Shop across the street.

"Amber, are you free?"

The pretty platinum blond manicurist, Bakersville's reigning rodeo queen, looked up. "Hi, Angie. Yeah, I can squeeze you in. Manicure?"

"Mani and pedi. It's been a day."

Amber motioned her over to her table. "What's going on? Deb didn't have what you were looking for?"

Angie noted the sarcasm in Amber's voice but decided to ignore it. She had bigger fish to fry. "Deb never has what I'm looking for, but that's not the main problem." She sighed. "My father thinks I need riding lessons."

Amber picked up her cuticle nippers. "I thought you knew how to ride."

"I do. Sort of. I just haven't done it in a while. I was good enough to do the rodeo queen patterns a million years ago, but I was just never that into it. I'm not Catie."

"Catie's a natural."

"Totally. Did you hear she's pregnant again?"

"Yeah, she stopped in yesterday and told me. I'm so happy for her and Chad."

"Yeah, me too." At least she wanted to be. But Catie's pregnancy only reminded her of her own biological clock. Her baby sister would be a mother before she would. Not that she had any grand desire to be a mother. At least that's what she kept telling herself.

Hell, how did I get on this subject?

"Can we get back to my riding?"

"Sure. You brought up Catie being pregnant."

Oh yeah. "I know. But right now this riding thing is driving me nuts."

"Riding is tough to learn, for sure, but there's nothing like it. I love it myself."

"Maybe you could teach me then."

Amber laughed. "Me? Are you kidding? I can get around, but I'm not qualified to instruct anyone."

Crap. Oh well. She'd approached a few local riding

instructors before Chad led her to Rafe Grayhawk. They'd all turned her down flat. Course she hadn't offered any of them a hundred bucks an hour, but they'd all seemed eager to tell her how they were too busy to teach the older Bay daughter how to ride a horse properly. Was she that difficult?

"Do I have a...reputation in this town?" she asked Amber.

Amber's gaze was locked on Angie's cuticles. Was she deliberately avoiding eye contact?

"I'm not sure what you mean."

"I mean...as being...difficult to work with, or something?"

Amber cleared her throat. "You're not difficult with me. We get along great."

"I know. I guess I mean... Oh heck, I don't know what I mean."

Amber placed Angie's right hand into the little bowl of solution and grabbed her other. This time she didn't look away. "Do you want me to be honest with you?"

"Of course."

"You're a friend to me as well as a client, so I don't want this to hurt our relationship."

"It won't. I promise."

"Okay." Amber sighed. "People who get to know you generally like you. That's not the problem."

"What is, then?"

"Well, you don't get to know a lot of people, for one thing. There are people you feel are..."

"Are what? What are you trying to say, Amber?"

"Let's put it this way. Would we be friends if I weren't friends with your sister? Would you have bothered getting to know me?"

"Of course. You're the best manicurist Judy's ever hired."

"That's not what I mean."

"What do you mean then?"

Amber sighed. "Sure, you'd let me do your nails. That's one thing. But would we hang out together during happy hour at The Bullfrog? Would we spend the day in Denver shopping?"

Angie bit her lip. Amber had a point. She'd never made friends with her manicurist before.

"And there's another thing."

God. "What?"

"No one wants to work for you."

"What do you mean? You work for me."

"I do your nails. Judy does your hair. We don't teach you to ride."

"I don't see what the difference is."

"We pamper you." Amber let out a giggle. "You're very good at being pampered. You won't get any pampering learning to ride. Riding is hard work. Don't get me wrong. I love it. The rewards are great. But you will not be pampered."

Angie's hackles rose. Who did Amber think she was? "It sounds like you're saying I'm spoiled."

Amber concentrated on the cuticles again. "You asked me to be honest, and you said it wouldn't harm our relationship."

"So you're admitting it? You think I'm spoiled?"

"I think you're a great person. I like you. We're friends, remember?"

"So I'm not spoiled?"

Amber started filing, still averting her gaze. "Let's put it this way. Remember a couple months ago when Judy added a touch too much red to your hair color?"

Angie remembered well. She'd looked like Elmo. "Yeah, I vaguely recall it."

"You called her incompetent and threatened to put her out of business. Never mind that she fixed your hair that same day, free of charge."

Warmth flooded to Angie's cheeks. *Yes, I overreacted.* "I apologized for that."

"I know you did, and Judy's still happy to have your business."

"She's the best hairdresser in this town."

"That she is. You knew it then, too."

Angie stiffened in her chair. "But demanding excellence doesn't mean I'm spoiled."

"No, it doesn't," Amber agreed. "But throwing a fit when you don't get it does."

Did I really throw a fit? She sighed. *Yeah, I did. Poor Judy. It's a wonder she still lets me back in her shop.*

Determination gripped her. The town of Bakersville would see a new Angelina Bay. She'd learn to ride as well as Catie, and she'd do it without throwing a single tantrum.

Well, she'd try, anyway.

"Do you know a ranch hand at Catie's named Rafe Grayhawk?"

Amber smiled. "Yeah, I've met him a few times. He's a hottie."

Hottie? That term didn't do Rafe Grayhawk justice. Angie hadn't been able to take her eyes off the tall, broad-shouldered man. The streams of sunlight through the boards on the barn ceiling had cast little highlights of indigo onto his long black hair. He'd worn a checkered shirt rolled up at the sleeves, and those forearms as they curried the horse...so sexy. His jeans clung just loosely enough over what she knew must be a fantastic butt. Yeah, she was a butt girl.

Give me a nice tight ass over pecs any day.

Though she didn't mind pecs. What might Rafe look like without his shirt?

She imagined he smelled like the musky outdoors. Course, she hadn't been able to smell anything but horse this morning.

She shook her head to clear it. Gorgeous as he was, he'd been a jerk. Who did he think he was? *I am his employer's sister, for God's sake.*

"He's going to teach me to ride."

"Wow, really? He gives lessons?" Amber smiled as she massaged Angie's right forearm. "Come to think of it, I'm getting a little rusty. Could use a refresher course."

Something sharp cut into Angie's gut. A twinge of...what? Jealousy? Not possible. She had no interest in Rafe Grayhawk. He was way beneath her. So why did it bother her that Amber indicated an interest in him? Of course Amber was interested. She was female, she was straight, and she had a pulse. Who wouldn't be attracted to Rafe Grayhawk?

"You don't need a refresher course, rodeo queen. You ride great."

"Still, to spend some time in the company of that hunk—"

"He charges a hundred dollars an hour." That ought to get her.

"A hundred an hour? He must be damn good."

He'd better be.

She'd find out in the morning.

Early in the morning.

CHAPTER TWO

"You're late."

Angie glanced at her watch. "By seven minutes. It's still the butt crack of dawn."

"Get here on time tomorrow or we're done." Rafe eyed her up and down. "Jeans, good for a start. Get some riding tights with leather seat patches. Your posterior will thank you."

"My posterior? I have ridden before, you know."

"When? For the rodeo queen shindig?"

God, that was fourteen years ago now. She grinned. She'd been crowned Bakersville's youngest rodeo queen at a mere eighteen years of age. But she'd ridden since then. Hadn't she?

"I guess it's been a while."

"Then trust me, you need the leather padding." He continued his assessment. "Boots—good, but clearly not broken in. Don't you have any work boots?"

"These *are* my work boots."

He shook his head. Was that an eye roll? He'd better learn to take her seriously.

"That looks like a nice shirt, too. It's fine for riding, but I suggest an older one tomorrow. You're going to get dirty."

Dirty? Angie's shirt was a western-style red cotton. She'd been sure it was the right choice. "So you want me to dress like trash, is that it?"

"Call it what you want, but you'll be happy enough when your clothes are slick with sweat and grime."

"I do not sweat."

He laughed. He actually laughed at her!

"Honey, when I'm done with you, you'll be sweatin' like a pig."

Like a pig? How rude. "I'm not your honey."

"Yeah, yeah. What about a helmet?"

"A helmet? Seriously? I'm not a complete beginner."

"Have you ridden this horse before?"

"No."

"Then you need a helmet. Have one tomorrow, honey."

"I said I'm not your honey." She stomped her foot to make her point and then shuffled it back. No need to get her dander up. Calling her honey was not likely to be the only thing Rafe did to tick her off today.

"You're right about that one. I suppose we should get started. By the end of today, you'll wish you'd gone for older clothes. Your horse is in the third stall from the left. Check her out, and then get her ready to ride."

Angie walked to Belle's stall. She was a beautiful mare, black as midnight with one lone white spot on her forehead. Angie ran her hand through her sleek mane. It was a little knotted. The horse looked fine, though. She walked back to join Rafe.

"She looks great. She's ready to ride."

Rafe's head tilted back and a boorish guffaw emerged from his throat. His Adam's apple bobbed as he laughed.

"What is it now?" Yes, her tone was a bit indignant. Why shouldn't it be?

"It's six o'clock in the morning. She hasn't been groomed yet. You do know how to groom her, don't you?"

Groom her? The hands did the grooming at Cha Cha, her

parents' ranch. At least she thought they did. Didn't they?

"Isn't that your job?"

"My job? Your sister comes in every morning and grooms Ladybird. In fact, I expect her any time now."

"I'm not my sister. I think she prefers horses to people sometimes. She thought she *was* a horse till she was about five years old."

That got another smile out of Rafe. Clearly, he was fond of Catie. But back to business.

"I'm paying you to teach me to ride, not groom."

"I'm paid to take care of Chad and Catie's horses. Belle is yours. She's not going anywhere till you get her properly groomed. Start with her feet."

"Her feet?"

"Christ, am I going to have to teach you everything?"

Her dander rose. Smoke might ooze out her ears any minute now. "For a hundred bucks an hour you ought to teach me to fly to the moon."

"Heck, I'd launch the rocket myself. Jesus. Come on." He walked toward Belle's stall.

She had no choice but to follow. Daddy had been adamant about her learning to ride. Why now? She had no idea. She'd been set to inherit her half of Bay Crossing, their ranch on the western slope, for over a decade. She'd found that out during her ill-fated engagement to Chad's brother Zach years ago. Zach was now happily married with a four-year-old rug rat, while Angie's biological clock whispered *ticktock, ticktock.*

She let out a breath. *Not going there right now.* She had horse feet to...what? Clean? Guess she'd find out.

She entered the stall and found Rafe running his left hand down Belle's left foreleg. "Up," he said, and Belle lifted her foot.

In his other hand he held what looked like a toothbrush with a metal hook attached. "This is a hoof pick. Use it to pry out any rocks or dirt in the hoof." He examined the foot. "I don't see any rocks. There's a little dirt." He brushed the hoof and a few small clumps of dirt fell onto the floor. "Come closer and look."

Angie knelt down next to Rafe.

"Her hoof looks good, but see here?" He pointed to the part not covered by the horseshoe. "The sole is more tender than the outside of the hoof. This darkish part is the frog. Belle's is healthy. This is what it's supposed to look like, so if the color changes or she has any lacerations, no matter how tiny, take note. A horse can't do its job if its feet are sore."

"Its job?"

"Carry you around while you learn to ride, of course." He put the hoof down. "Your turn. Her right foreleg. Come on."

Angie hedged a little. "What if she kicks me?"

"You plan to do anything to make her kick you? You just saw me do it. She's used to having her feet cleaned. Run your left hand down her leg so you can brush out the foot with your right."

"I'm left-handed."

"Fine. Just do the opposite then. Here, I'll show you."

He took her right hand, and a tingle shot up her arm. She jolted. She hadn't felt anything like that in a long time. But Rafe Grayhawk? He was a god to look at, but not her type at all.

Belle's foreleg was sleek and soft. "Up," she said, as Rafe had, and miracle of miracles, Belle lifted her hoof. Angie brushed away some dirt and examined the sole and frog carefully. They looked identical to the first.

"See anything?" Rafe asked.

"No. She looks fine."

"Good job. Now the hind legs."

Angie repeated the process twice more and pronounced Belle's hooves healthy.

"Now get the currycomb," Rafe said. "You do know which one is the currycomb, right?"

"Yes, I know what a currycomb is." She wasn't a complete imbecile. She grabbed the round instrument and started on Belle's left side, circling the brush in small movements through the horse's coat.

"Very nice. You do know a little something."

Yes, she knew how to curry. Her 4-H days hadn't been a complete waste. After she became rodeo queen at eighteen, though, she'd left animal care to the hands. Belle stood still, snorting every now and then. "You like that, girl?"

"Most horses enjoy grooming if it's done properly," Rafe said. "Take a look at her body while you're doing it. See if she has any injuries we should be aware of. Be sure to lighten your touch in the bony areas around her shoulders so you don't hurt her. Here, let me show you."

He took the currycomb from her, and this time, despite the smell of barn, she caught a quick whiff of his scent. Leather, the outdoors, and something unique that she couldn't quite put her finger on. Was it coconut? Couldn't be. A chill feathered up her spine, but disappeared as quickly as it came.

What amazing forearms this man had. The sinewy muscles contracted as he showed her how to brush Belle's bonier areas.

"Gentle, see? She likes that."

"Let me try." Angie took the comb from him. Was she actually enjoying this process?

After currying came combing out the tangles in Belle's

mane. The poor thing did have some knots. She started at the bottom, disentangling the strands until she could move upward. She had a flashback of combing through her sister's long hair when Catie was six and Angie was seventeen. Catie used to scream bloody murder. Belle took it a lot better as Angie detangled her tail.

Next, Rafe showed her how to use the body brush to get what the currycomb missed. Belle seemed to enjoy the long, sweeping strokes. What the currycomb had loosened, this brush swept away. Angie sneezed when some dirt flew up her nose.

"Here." Rafe handed her a red bandana. "Get used to sneezing in here, especially if you're sensitive to dust and pollen. Horses carry all kinds of things in their coats."

She wiped her nose and face. Grime dirtied the crimson of the bandana. She looked down. Rafe had been right. She was filthy. She shook her head. Older clothes tomorrow.

With the finer bristled finishing brush, Rafe showed Angie how to clean the horse's face, ears, and throat, and then do the body again to give her a radiant sheen.

"Time for grooming spray?" Angie asked.

"No grooming spray." Rafe took the finishing brush from her and examined her job. "It's not necessary, and it sometimes makes the coat slick. Not a good thing for beginning riders."

"I'm not exactly a beginner."

"You're close enough. Personally, I don't think horses need any of those products on their hair or skin. I don't like hoof ointment either." He handed her a damp sponge. "Clean around her eyes and muzzle. How do her eyes look?"

"They look fine to me."

"No tearing or anything?"

"Nope."

"Good. Belle seems to be in excellent health. She'll be ready to ride tomorrow."

Excuse me? "Tomorrow? What do you think I got up for today?"

"For a lesson. You learned how to groom your horse before a ride. Sorry, but it took a little longer than I expected. I figured you'd know how to groom. I've got stock to feed and then a couple errands I'm running for Chad."

"But how am I supposed to learn to ride if you don't—"

"Teach you? Honey, I taught you what any good instructor would on your first lesson. Be here at six sharp tomorrow. We'll get her groomed faster, and I'll have more time to get you up on that horse. Today's lesson is over."

"But—"

Rafe walked out of the barn, his jeans loosely moving around the curves of his muscular ass. Left her standing in Belle's stall, the sponge still in her hand, watching him walk away.

And wondering what that ass looked like without the covering.

★ ★ ★

"Hey, Annie." Rafe entered the office of Annie McCray, the town veterinarian and the wife of the oldest McCray brother, Dallas.

"Hi there," Annie said in her spicy New Jersey accent. "How're you doing, Rafe?"

"Good. Tom texted me and said he forgot to leave you the rent check. I can write you one now if you want."

"No problem. Just have him leave it tomorrow."

"Okay, thanks. Chad needs some antibiotics for a couple of the steers. Said you'd know which ones."

"Yep, I've got them right here. They just came in an hour ago." She pulled a package out from under her counter and wiped her brow. "Sheesh, it's hot."

The late August day was balmy, but not overly so. "You feeling all right?"

"Oh yeah, I'm fine. Just flashing a little just like the first time. I guess you haven't heard the news. Dallas and I are expecting again."

"Really? Congratulations. Catie is expecting too."

"Yeah, that's something else, isn't it? These cousins'll be almost exactly the same age." She sat down in the waiting area. "I've got two more appointments today. I wish I could just go on home."

"Can I get you something? I can run over to Rena's for an iced herbal tea."

"You're a sweetheart, but no, I'm fine. I'm sure you have things to do."

"I've got a few more errands here in town, and then some projects back at the ranch I need to get moving on today. My time is limited now that I'm doing freelance work."

"Freelance work?"

"I'm teaching Angelina Bay"—why did his groin pulse at the mention of her name?—"how to ride."

"Angie? No kidding?"

Angie? Didn't seem to suit her. She was an "Angelina" all the way. Condescending and a genuine pain in the ass.

Angelina.

Angelina naked. In the shower. Shiny rivers of water

meandering over her curvy body.

He shook his head slightly to clear the unwanted image. "Yeah. Can you believe I only just met her?"

Annie chuckled. "Yeah, I can believe it. She's not the type to mingle with the ranch hands."

"That's the truth. What is with her, anyway?"

"She's all right, just spoiled as all get out. She used to be friends with Dallas's bitch of an ex-wife, and a more spoiled brat doesn't exist on this planet than Chelsea. Since Chelsea's been gone, Angie's been a little better. I get along with her fine, though I can tell my Jersey accent grates on her." Annie smiled and lifted one black eyebrow. "So I make sure to really emphasize it when I'm around her."

Rafe laughed. "I found out today she's a lot older than Catie. I wouldn't have guessed."

"The years have definitely been kind to her. How are your lessons going?"

"We've only had one so far. Okay, I guess."

"Well, don't let her get to you. She's a good person inside. Sometimes it's just hard to see under all the fluff."

Underneath that fluff was one sexy woman.

If only he could stop picturing her naked.

CHAPTER THREE

"Daddy, all we did was groom the horse today. He didn't teach me anything."

Wayne Bay sat behind the desk in his home office and regarded his daughter. She'd been his little princess for so long. Catie hadn't come along until eleven years later, and she'd been more of a tomboy who preferred to hang out with the horses in the barn, so Angie had still been the jewel of his eye.

He'd been scared to death when she was born a month early, but she'd come out over seven pounds and strong as an ox, screaming bloody murder. He promised her the world that day, and he'd done everything within his power to deliver. Every day she'd grown more beautiful, more intelligent, more strong-willed, and every day she wormed her way further into his heart. His little princess.

Yes, he'd spoiled her. He'd enjoyed every minute of it. But he'd done her a disservice. Here she was, thirty-two years old, single, without any marketable skills, and about to inherit half a ranch.

"Grooming is a must before riding, princess."

"But we didn't ride at all!"

"Grayhawk knows what he's doing."

"I hope you're right, Daddy. I hate getting up so early."

"Getting up early is part of running a ranch."

"Isn't that what the hands are for? Honestly, what is the point of being the owner then? Why not just be a hand?"

Wayne widened his eyes. Was this really how he'd raised his daughter? To be a snob? How had that happened? Catie and Harper, his son and Angelina's brother, weren't spoiled like this. He'd truly ruined his little girl.

Well, no longer.

"Princess, it's high time you learned more than just riding. After your lesson tomorrow, you're spending the day with me. You'll shadow me, and I'll show you exactly what's involved in owning a beef ranch."

"Wayne."

He looked up to see his wife in the doorway. How long had she been there?

"We have an appointment tomorrow, remember?"

He sighed. "Right. Sorry, I forgot." He turned back to Angie. "The next day then. Or better yet, you can follow Harper around tomorrow. He does the same stuff I do. He'll teach you what running a ranch is all about."

"Daddy, come on. Isn't getting up at the crack of dawn to groom a horse enough?"

"Not even slightly," Wayne said. "Now go on. I need to talk to your mother."

Angie left the room, pouting.

"What are we going to do with her, Maria?" he asked his wife. "She's acting like a three-year-old. How did we let this happen? Our other two children are hard workers and understand what goes into ranching."

"You spoiled her, Wayne," Maria said, "and I went along with it. We're both to blame."

Wayne slowly let out a breath. "I suppose so. The question is can we fix it?"

Maria walked behind him and rubbed his shoulders. Even

having the tension kneaded out of his sore muscles didn't relax him.

"We can fix it," Maria said. "We don't have a choice. But Wayne, we need to tell her."

Wayne shook his head. "No. Not yet. Not until it's absolutely necessary."

"It's necessary now."

Wayne pounded the desk with his fist. "No. This is my decision, not yours."

Maria said nothing and continued to massage his neck.

Wayne closed his eyes. Decisions, decisions. Why so many decisions, when all he wanted to do was not think at all?

★ ★ ★

"Catie?" Angie entered her sister's ranch house. "You home?"

Chad and Catie's black lab, Marnie, greeted her with wagging tail and tongue. Angie gave her a pet. "Hi there, girl. Where's your mama?"

A quick walk through the living area to the kitchen proved neither Chad nor Catie was home. Angie sauntered out back to the pool house and changed into her red bikini. She loved Chad and Catie's pool. It was twice the size of the Bays'. A swim and some relaxing sun time would rev her up for the next day of rising at dawn, a riding lesson, and shadowing Harper all day.

Usually a morning of shopping and pampering sufficed to rev her up. Strange that it didn't do the trick today. She dismissed the nagging thought.

Damn! She was thirty-two years old. She didn't have to do what her daddy said. No way would she trail Harper around tomorrow. In fact, she might blow off her riding lesson, too.

She pulled a *chaise longue* poolside, spread a beach towel on the chair, and lay down. Nothing like the Colorado rays.

And nothing burned her fair skin like the Colorado rays. She went back to the pool house, grabbed some 30 SPF sunscreen, and sat back down in her chair. She loosened her straps and started smoothing the lotion over her shoulders.

"Need some help?"

She looked up into the black eyes of Rafe Grayhawk. What was a hand doing by Chad's pool? And why did he look so lusciously yummy in those low-slung jeans and a black muscle shirt?

"Thank you, but—" *Dear God, he's gorgeous.*

His long ebony hair was pulled back in a low ponytail, and he'd tied a blue bandana around his head like a do-rag. She hadn't seen his upper arms and shoulders before. They were sleek, bronze, and muscular, a perfect match to those exquisite forearms. And his hands... She'd seen them up close this morning. They were large, strong, capable hands. Hands that were no doubt equally at home handling a horse and pleasuring a woman—both with ease.

The afternoon sun blazed over her skin even as tingles erupted beneath it. Hot and cold...delicious sensations.

How would those hands feel rubbing sunscreen on her back?

Only one way to find out. She cleared her throat. "On second thought, I could use some help after all. I always miss a spot on my back."

"I can't. I'm on the clock. I just stopped by to leave some stuff for Chad."

"Then why did you offer?"

His lips parted. Was he going to smile?

Nope.

"I offered because I figured there wasn't a snowball's chance in hell you'd ever take me up on it. After all, I'm nothing but a hand."

Her heart lurched. His deep voice resonated with disdain. Disdain for her. Had Amber been right? Was she nothing more than a spoiled brat who considered herself above everyone else? Then again, she *was* set to inherit half a ranch on the western slope. She'd been born into a well-respected family. Where did Rafe live? He didn't live on the ranch in one of the houses hands sometimes rented. That much she knew.

Heck, what did it matter? Right now, this moment, she wanted his hands on her. It had been such a long time since a man had touched her...so very long.

"You made an offer, Mr. Grayhawk, whether you were serious or not. And I accepted."

"I withdrew the offer."

"I accepted before you withdrew. Now we have a contract."

He rubbed the side of his face. "A contract? For putting on suntan lotion? Are you kiddin'?"

"Absolutely not. If you don't perform, I can sue you for breach of contract."

"Yeah, yeah, I know your brother's a lawyer. Catie told me. And even a 'hand' like me knows oral contracts are binding. But, Angelina—"

"Angie."

"Angie, then." He shook his head. "Doesn't sound right."

"It's what everyone calls me."

"Fine. Angie. You and I both know this isn't a good idea." He smirked. "And it'd never hold up in court."

"Do you really want to take that chance?" Angie pasted her best seductive smile on her face.

He smiled and a dimple appeared on his left cheek. The ice around her heart started to crack as he sauntered toward her, his hand out.

On instinct, she reached out and touched her fingertips to his.

"I was reaching for the sunscreen," he said.

"Oh." More warmth flooded her already flaming cheeks. How needy was she? She placed the bottle of lotion in his brown hand. "My back, please." She lay face down on her chaise.

The chair dipped a bit when he sat on the edge. "I'll need to move your straps if you want good coverage."

She shuddered when his fingers brushed her skin, and hoped he didn't notice. "By all means."

Smooth hands, silky lotion, hot man. It had been so, so long. Her nipples hardened into nubs and threatened to poke through the chaise. His sensual strokes warmed her through and through. The tickle between her legs became more intense. From a back rub? That had never happened before.

Course never before had she gotten a backrub from the amazing Rafe Grayhawk.

Fierce need flooded her. She wanted him, desired him, might die if she didn't get just a smidge of him. Before she had time to change her mind, she flipped over onto her back, her bare breasts exposed to his view.

His eyebrows shot to his forehead. "Uh—"

Without thinking, only feeling, she pulled him toward her until his lips crushed against hers.

The kiss of a century...how wonderful, his soft sweet lips,

so delectable against her own. Was it a hint of lime? Couldn't be. Such a man as Rafe Grayhawk wouldn't wear flavored lip balm. Millimeter by millimeter she feasted on those luscious lips, kissing first the top and then the bottom, running her tongue over their plumpness and plunging it inside to taste him. He kissed her back, swirling his tongue around hers in a playful manner that didn't seem quite "him." Yet it was. He nipped at her, tugged on her lower lip. Her sex pulsed between her legs. She was vaguely aware of her hips moving upward, down again, upward, downward. God, how she wanted him.

Her nipples strained against...nothing. Nothing covered them. What had she been thinking? But oh, she couldn't think. She could only feel. Feel his chest lowering onto hers, the brush of his cotton muscle shirt against her hard nubs. Surely he could feel them poking into his chest. If only he'd lose the shirt...

He groaned into her mouth and moved his lips to her cheek, raining tiny kisses along the way.

"You taste just like a tequila sunrise. Sweet and tangy." He nibbled on her shoulder.

Goose bumps erupted over her body. Her breasts ached. Her nipples tingled. "Oh my God," Angie said, her voice a whisper. "My nipples. Please."

He trailed his lips over her chin, along the contours of her neck and shoulders, until they lightly brushed one nipple.

She jolted. Tiny shivers skittered across her skin and landed between her legs.

How long had it been? Years. Four? Five years? Back when she was engaged to Zach McCray.

Her vibrator helped, but even Mr. Ace was no substitute for a living and breathing male.

A beautiful Native American male, with skin the color of bronze and eyes dark as midnight. And full pink lips that nibbled on her nipple as though he were starving and it was a feast. How she wanted those lips kissing and sucking the most secret part of her.

She spread her legs. Was that involuntary? No, because she knew she was doing it. And she knew why.

"Touch me," she whispered. "Please."

His lips still clamped on her nipple, he lightly brushed his fingertips over the indentation of her waist and over her hips. He nudged her bikini bottom aside. She twitched.

God, yes. Please.

One long finger breached her, and a heavy sigh escaped her throat. So good. So very, very good.

He let her nipple tumble from his lips. "You're so wet, baby. So fucking wet."

She raised her hips as he slowly slid his finger in and out of her heat. How had she gone so long without this? How?

Right now, she'd willingly give anything, anything at all, to have his hardness embedded inside her. Would it be bronze and beautiful like the rest of him? Would he sink into her slowly or would he plunge in, desperate to be part of her?

He kissed her nipple again, a tiny peck, looked up at her, and smiled, his pearly teeth a beautiful contrast against his dark skin. "I bet you're sweet. Damn, I'd love to taste you."

Those lips between her legs? That tongue? She'd die an untimely death. *Do I want his lips or his cock?* She could no doubt have both, but which did she want first?

She didn't have to make that decision.

In a flash, he withdrew his finger and abruptly stood.

"God, Angelina, I'm so sorry."

Sorry? Was he kidding? "What for?"

"This is your sister's house. My boss's house. And you're a client of mine. What the hell am I doing?"

Sweat beaded on his brow, and his arousal was apparent beneath his jeans. Again, she wondered what he looked like in all his glory. And how his glory would feel inside her wet heat that still throbbed.

He grabbed the bandana off his head and wiped his forehead. He penetrated her with his gaze. "What was I thinking? I don't even..."

"Even what?" Angie asked.

He shook his head. "Nothing. I got work to do." He turned and walked around the side of the house, disappearing from her view.

Angie sat, her breasts still bare, her sex still aching. She flung her bikini top onto the deck, stood, and walked to the side of the pool.

She dived in.

Nope, still didn't cool her off.

★ ★ ★

"I need some sex."

Amber and Catie both shot liquid out of their mouths, Amber a pink cosmo and Catie a virgin pina colada. Happy hour at the Bullfrog on a Thursday night. Angie had dragged Catie out and they'd picked up Amber on the way. After fifteen minutes of small talk and one martini, Angie let loose with her bomb.

"Don't we all." Amber turned to Catie. "Not all of us are lucky enough to have a McCray warming our bed at night."

"I could have had a McCray—" Nope, she couldn't have. Zach McCray had never loved her. Their engagement had been finagled by their two mothers, best friends who wanted to see their ranches combined. Laurie McCray had passed on over a year ago. Angie's mother still missed her.

How had she gone this long without a relationship? Without male companionship? She'd dated, but none of them had lived up to her expectations. Always something from her list crept up.

Ever since the Zach debacle, she'd wanted more—a real connection—so she'd made a list of characteristics for her ideal man. Catie made no secret of her feelings that her sister was being ridiculous, and gave her crap about "Angie's list" on a regular basis.

Angie had thought Zach possessed it all. Intelligence— he was a Harvard man. Movie star good looks—one brown eye and one blue eye might make a normal person look odd, but heterochromia worked on him. A boatload of money—the McCrays owned the biggest beef ranch in Colorado. What he hadn't given her was love and devotion. Problem was, because of her list of standards, no one had lived up to Zach McCray since, so Angie never kept anyone around long enough to see if love was even possible.

But what was wrong with having standards? She perused her list in her mind.

1. Financially affluent
2. Intelligent, with an IQ in the superior range at least, preferably genius range
3. No past marriages
4. Ambition

5. Wants children

6. Adores me

7. Good-looking with a great body

8. No fear of commitment

Only eight items and she'd kept the looks down at number seven. That had to prove she wasn't completely shallow. Seriously, what was wrong with wanting the best?

Angie didn't want to settle. Her mother had settled. Wayne had married Maria after she'd gotten pregnant with Angie. Their marriage had sustained itself and they produced two more children. They owned two ranches. But Maria had freely admitted to both her daughters that they'd never been in love. They liked each other. Respected each other. Worked well as partners.

But no spark.

Angie wanted spark.

The sparks between her and Rafe Grayhawk this afternoon could have ignited a freaking forest fire.

Sex with Zach McCray had been great, no doubt. But he'd never adored her. She chuckled out loud as she realized why she hadn't had sex since Zach and the creation of the list. Sex wasn't even *on* the list! She only now realized it. All the guys failed one or more items on the list before sex even came into consideration.

Okay, new item on the list.

9. Great in bed

In fact, she'd move that to number one. No way was she going another five years without sex. She was thirty-two.

Things might start to atrophy.

"Dump the list, Angie," Catie was saying. "It's the only way. Or have a few one-night stands if it's just the sex you want."

She'd come darn close to that with Rafe. A one-night stand—or rather a one-afternoon stand—had never been her style. Yet today she'd been ready to chuck it all and screw Rafe right on her sister's deck. How completely slutty. The town might have a few things to say about Angelina Bay, but no one had ever accused her of being a slut.

"One-night stands are not my style," she said.

"Have you ever had one?" Amber asked.

She shook her head.

"Then how do you know?"

She cracked a smile. "I guess I don't. And I know Catie doesn't either since Chad's her one and only. Why don't you tell us about one-night stands, Amber?"

Amber's cheeks pinked. "They're not really my style either, though I'll admit to two of them. Both were back in San Antonio. I was pretty drunk during the first one, though at least I was lucid enough to make sure he used a condom. The second one was shortly before I came here. I met this totally hot guy at a bar a few nights before I left. Damon was his name. I never found out his last name. Blond, blue-eyed, and gorgeous. We went to his place and humped like bunnies all night. In the morning, he kissed me goodbye and I left. We didn't exchange numbers or anything."

Angie looked around the Bullfrog. Joe Bradley, the mechanic, sat with Sheriff Doug Cartright and the very married Dallas McCray. The rest of the crowd was younger. Not really any one-night stand material. Well, what did she expect on a Thursday night in Bakersville, Colorado? Hardly a thriving metropolis.

Didn't matter anyway. The only one-night stand she wanted was with Rafe Grayhawk, and he'd turned her down.

Angie Bay didn't usually get turned down. She did the turning down. Clearly she'd done way too much of that lately.

"God, I need some sex," she said again.

"You're sounding really desperate," Amber said. "Exactly how long has it been for you?"

"Over five years."

Catie and Amber spat their drinks again.

"The way my friends keep showering me, we're going to need more drinks over here," Angie said to the bartender.

"You haven't had sex since Zach?" Catie shook her head.

"You've seen the list. I have standards."

"Having standards for a relationship is one thing," Amber said. "Sex is another thing."

"I'm not sure I agree," Catie said.

"You found your one and only love when you were five," Amber said. "That's great, but most of us aren't so lucky. And it's fun to test the waters sometimes."

Oh, I had some serious fun testing the waters this afternoon.

Amber took a sip of her cosmo, this time without a spit take. "How are we going to get you some?"

"I'm sorry," Catie chimed in, "but I refuse to help my sister get some. It's...weird."

"You're getting it on a regular basis from one of Bakersville's prime studs." Amber smiled. "Have some pity here. Angie needs a little nookie."

Catie laughed at that. "Nookie? Well, okay. What about Joe or Doug over there? They're both good-looking. Joe's a great guy. Doug's a little bit of a lech, but hey, if it's sex you want."

"Joe's always greasy."

"He's a mechanic."

"And Doug. I don't like redheads."

"His hair's more auburn," Amber said, "though I agree with Catie. He's a lech. Steer clear. Joe, though, is a sweetie. I'm surprised someone hasn't grabbed him yet. Word around the beauty shop is that he's one of the town's two most eligible bachelors now that all the McCrays have been snapped up."

"Yeah? Who's the other?" Angie asked.

Amber laughed. "No one who would interest you. Your brother."

Catie guffawed into her virgin drink. "Harp? He's a hottie of the town?"

"Heck, yeah," Amber said. "He's good-looking, educated, has money. Best of all, he's a nice guy."

Angie raised her eyebrows. "Harper's good-looking?"

"Uh, *yeah*. He's a male version of the two of you put together. Aren't there women crawling all over him?"

"No, not really... Hey, aren't we here to discuss my sex life?" Angie speared one of the olives in her second martini. "And I draw the line at my own brother, thanks."

"Okay." Amber set her empty glass on the counter. "Here's what you do." She paused.

"What? Don't leave me hanging here."

"Chuck the list."

"I have to agree, Angie," Catie said. "That list has gotten you nowhere. Sheesh, no sex in five years? Was Zach McCray that hard to live up to?"

"No, it's just..." What was it exactly? Why was she so picky?

"I'm tellin' you," Amber said. "Try a one-night stand. You'll be a new woman."

"Okay." Angie set her drink down with such gusto an olive flopped onto the counter. "I'll do it."

And she already knew exactly who she wanted to "do it" with.

CHAPTER FOUR

"Angelina."

He never called her Angelina. Sometimes Angie. Usually princess. Her father's voice was stern. She'd heard him use that tone with Harper many times, and even with Catie once or twice. But never with her. Never with Daddy's little princess.

She drew in a deep breath and regarded her father's handsome face. Was he looking older? His hair was mostly white now, but his face had always looked young. Did his cheeks seem a little more hollow? She'd seen him inside way too much lately. He must be spending too much time in the office. He needed to be outside more, doing the ranch work he loved.

"Yes, Daddy?"

"I hear from Harper you were nowhere to be found today."

God. "Yes, well, I wasn't feeling all that well. And really, I don't see the need to shadow Harper to learn about ranching. I'll just read a book or something."

"Shadowing Harper today was not a request. You may be well over the age of majority, but you're still living on my ranch. It's time you starting earning your keep."

"Daddy, I have my own little house."

"For which you pay no rent. Harper pays his own way around here, and so did your sister until she got married."

Angie huffed. "Catie spent the last four years in Paris, for God's sake."

"Getting her education. Before that, ever since she was old enough to lift a currycomb, she's been pulling her weight."

"I got an education too, you know."

"Yes, and it's high time you used it. It was so long ago, what was your major again? Home Ec or some other froufrou thing?"

She cleared her throat. Why was he thinking the worst of her? She had a brain. There was a reason she wanted an intelligent man. Her own IQ was quite high.

"Health sciences, with a minor in biology."

"Good, good. With a biology background you can start taking more responsibility for the health and nutrition of the animals."

"College was long ago, Daddy. I'll have to read up."

"So be it. Get online and find what you need. And I expect you to show up tomorrow and work with Harper."

She rolled her eyes. "Fine." She turned to leave.

"One more thing."

She turned back. "Yes?"

"Grayhawk tells me you didn't show up for your lesson this morning."

She'd meant to, but she'd gotten to bed late after hanging at the Bullfrog. She hadn't been able to force herself out of bed this morning. Plus—her neck warmed—she was embarrassed to see him after their little interlude at Catie's pool.

"I'm sorry. I overslept."

He cleared his throat and his nose reddened.

Uh-oh. Wayne Bay with a red nose was not a good thing.

"I'll see that you get an alarm clock," he said through clenched teeth. "And just so we understand each other, there's one other thing."

"What, Daddy?"

He shuffled some papers on his desk. "This"—he held up a document—"is my original last will and testament, leaving Bay Crossing to you and Catie and Cha Cha to Harper." He set the papers down and held up what appeared to be an identical document. "This is a *new* will Harper just drew up for me."

"Why do you need a new will?"

"Why don't you take a look at it?" He handed her the document.

She hadn't been to law school like her brother, but she was capable of reading a will. Everything looked in order, until—

Her skin chilled as anger welled within her. "What? You can't possibly be serious!"

"I'm completely serious, Angelina. You have not demonstrated that you are capable of owning one of my properties when I'm gone. You either show me you're serious and learn about ranching, or I leave Bay Crossing solely to Catie."

Not only would she not get her share of the ranch, but she'd get nothing whatsoever. None of the money in the bank, none of her mother's jewelry, not even Nana's afghan—nothing, nothing, and more nothing.

"This is completely unfair! How can you even think of doing this?"

"I've protected you far too long, Angelina. I finally see that I haven't done you any favors. You either learn ranching or go on your merry way and find something else to do and someone else to finance your lifestyle. I won't be your sugar daddy any longer."

"But—"

"No buts. Do not miss any more riding lessons with

Grayhawk, either. Chad is doing me a huge favor by letting him take time out of his duties to teach you."

"It's not exactly a favor. Chad has tons of hands, and Rafe is being well paid."

"Yes. By me. May I remind you that you have *nothing?*"

Angie's throat constricted. Had someone punched her in the belly? Sure felt like it. Tears welled in the corners of her eyes.

"Daddy..."

"Crying won't work on me anymore. I've said my piece and I meant every word. Now go on. You have a busy day tomorrow."

★ ★ ★

"You had to do it, Wayne," Maria Bay said to her husband.

He nodded. "I know. It was just so much damn harder than I thought it would be. I still see that sweet little girl in a pink dress."

"She's still your little girl. She always will be. But now she'll have a means of supporting herself."

"I don't have to do this. She'd easily have enough money to live on just with her profits from the ranching operations."

"But you said yourself when we started discussing this— she'd never grow. And that's not what we wanted for any of our children. No one handed anything to you. Why should you hand it to her?"

He raked his fingers through his hair. "I know, I know. I stand by the decision. This is my fault."

"You spoiled her. We both did. She was the first, and a girl. But stop blaming yourself. It's counterproductive. And it's wearing on you."

He sighed. She was right, of course. "I need to get to bed, Mia."

"I know. Come on."

★ ★ ★

Well, there she is.

Rafe blinked.

Was it a mirage? A sexy mirage with dark hair in two ponytails, and yes, it was true—actual worn cowboy boots? Still hadn't gotten the riding tights, but jeans would do. Jeans that fit her sweet little rump just right. He willed his groin not to respond.

Angie Bay was not only up and in the stall before he got there at six a.m., she had Belle almost ready. Too bad all deals were off.

"Morning." He tipped his cowboy hat.

"Good morning." She smiled as she ran the finishing brush over Belle's sleek ebony flank. "I'm all ready to get going."

"Sorry. You missed your lesson yesterday. We no longer have a deal."

"Yes, I know." She cleared her throat. "I'm sorry about that. I...er...wasn't feeling well."

"You could have called."

"Don't have your number."

"Give me your cell."

She handed it to him and he quickly programmed his number into it.

"There." He tossed it back to her. "Now no more excuses."

She smiled again. She sure was pretty as a fresh daisy this

morning. Had she had an attitude adjustment? Her scarlet lips curved up slightly higher on the right side, making her smile just a tad lopsided. The tiny imperfection made her all the more desirable.

Damn, those lips had tasted good. Like a tequila sunrise heavy on the grenadine. He could have kissed her into oblivion. Damn near had, until it dawned on him that he was close to fucking his boss's sister-in-law on his deck.

Good way to get fired. He needed his job here. Chad McCray paid well, and the extra for teaching Angelina to ride would come in handy too. Pretty soon his dad could go to Arizona. He wouldn't give up the extra dough. The opportunity to teach Angie had come along just at the right time. Bart over at the Bullfrog had offered him a job tending bar two nights a week for some extra cash. Now he didn't need to take that moonlighting job.

Though he did make a mean tequila sunrise.

Orange juice, tequila, and grenadine would taste great drizzled over Angie's sweet red nipples. Course they tasted amazing alone—he had firsthand knowledge of that. That soft little sigh from her throat as he tugged—

Damn, these jeans are tight.

"All right," he said. "Get her saddled up."

Angie's slender arms could barely lift the heavy saddle, but she managed to get it on Belle's back. In the meantime, Rafe saddled Adonis.

"Go ahead and give her a bit now, but eventually you won't be using reins much."

"What?" Angie's mouth dropped open.

"You'll be controlling the horse with your legs. It's a much better way for both of you."

"For her, maybe. Not for me. My legs aren't that strong."

He'd seen her legs two days previous. They looked plenty strong. Sturdy and shapely. She'd have no trouble learning to ride this way. And he'd enjoy watching that body develop into an equestrienne's. Fact of the matter he'd enjoy watching that body do just about anything.

She was lovely.

"Okay, honey, let's take them out."

They led the horses out of the stall and into one of the fenced training pastures.

"Now go ahead and mount her." He watched. "From the left side, good."

"Hey, look at me!" Angie smiled and raised one hand. "It's been a long time since I've been up here, it feels—"

Thunk. Rafe let out a laugh as Angie landed on her backside right on the grass.

"Ouch!"

"Now don't you wish you'd gotten those tights with leather patches?"

"Why on earth?"

"You slid right off the saddle, honey. I saw it comin' bright as day."

"You might have warned me."

"And miss this? I don't think so." He helped her to her feet. "You'll want to invest in one of those butt pillows, too. It'll help when you're trying to sit at dinner tonight."

"Butt pillow?"

"Sure. You've seen them. People use them for hemorrhoids."

She rubbed her ass cheeks. "You've got to be kidding."

"Can't say I am." He shook his head. "You're cute as hell,

you know that?"

Before he thought better of it, he pulled her to his body and crushed his lips to hers. He traced the seam of her lips with his tongue. "Yeah, baby, that's right. Open for me."

Her lips parted, and she still tasted of tequila sunrise—the tang of the orange juice, the smokiness of the tequila, the sweet cherry of grenadine—all together in Angelina Bay's kisses. Her tongue swooped out and met his, and suddenly the kiss had gone beyond anything he'd ever known. It was a joining, a searing, a complete union.

This, from a kiss?

Rather than stop him, the thought spurred him on. He kissed her more deeply, more intensely. His tongue learned the contours of her teeth, her gums, the inside of her cheeks. All sweetness, all Angelina. Her kisses drugged him with a narcotic he couldn't live without.

He ripped his mouth from hers. Couldn't live without? What kind of crazy nonsense was spewing inside his brain?

He'd only just met her, didn't even like her. Of course she was beautiful. No one could deny that. But he'd never been one to be swept away by physical beauty. What was so different now?

God, how I want another taste of her.

Her normally sparkling green eyes were glazed over. She blinked a few times. Her lips were beet red and swollen from his kisses.

Just one more—

This time she came to him. Angie flung her arms around his neck and she mashed her lips to his.

Damn it all—the kiss was even better than the first. She seduced him, tantalized him with her mouth. His cock hardened in his jeans and he pulled her close and ground it against her belly. His groan seemed to come from somewhere else.

Still the tequila sunrise—tangy, smoky, and sweet. That was Angie. That *was* Angie. Not just her kisses but all of her. Her tangy attitude, her smoky sexiness, and the sweetness she kept hidden until she wanted to let it out—like this morning when she got to the barn before he did and gave him a dazzling smile when he entered.

Angelina.

Angie.

Angel.

Oh, hell no.

Angie. It suited her now that he knew her slightly better.

Angie.

"Angie," he whispered against her lips.

"Hmm?"

"I want you."

"I want you too." Her voice was low and husky. "God, how I want you."

But they were in one of the training rings, out in plain sight, on his boss's property...his boss's sister-in-law. *God, I don't care. So don't care.*

"Let's get the horses back."

When Belle and Adonis had been secured in their stalls, he grabbed Angie's hand and led her to one of the small houses on the property.

"Where are we?"

"Gerry's on vacation this week in Denver, thank God. I'm taking care of his cat."

Where *was* the damn feline? *Who cares?* Right now his

only concern was where the bed was. Hell, he didn't even need a bed. The couch would do. Or the floor. Or the kitchen table...

He grabbed both her hands. "You still want this?"

"God, yes, Rafe. Please. I'm so wet for you."

His last resolve crumbled. Had it ever been there in the first place? He pulled her into the bedroom.

The cat lay on the bed. He shooed her away. All he wanted was Angie, naked, on this bed, gloving his cock in her slick, wet heat.

"Oh, baby," he said as he unbuttoned her shirt. There they were, those beautiful breasts, like two ripe peaches pushing out from the confines of her bra. He eased the cotton fabric from her shoulders and unclasped the bra. Her breasts fell gently against her chest. He cupped them, thumbed her nipples.

"Oh, yes," she breathed. "That feels so good, Rafe."

His name from her lips ignited flames in his loins.

"Yes," she said again.

"So beautiful," he said. "You like that, baby?"

"God, yes."

He fingered each nipple and lightly tugged on them.

"Rafe, suck them. Please."

"Since you said please..."

He bent down and placed a light kiss on one. Her response was immediate. It budded even harder against his lips. Her skin was like satin. No, silk. Fine Turkish silk. So soft and delicate.

He kissed the nipple again, twirled his tongue around it, and licked it. Her areola contracted, and he sucked the hard bud into his mouth.

"Ah, God." Her voice lowered an octave.

The raspy sultriness spurred him on. He sucked harder, all the while twirling the other nipple between his thumb and middle finger. He tugged it lightly, and then harder.

He could feast on these all day.

Angie's hips moved in slow circles. His free hand wandered to the juncture between her legs. He fondled her through her jeans, slowly circling.

Her hips and moans increased in tempo. "God, please," she said.

He fumbled with the snap and zipper of her jeans until they loosened, plunged his hand inside, and found her heat. *Wet.*

"So wet, baby. So wet for me."

She writhed against his hand. Though it pained him, he had to let her nipples go. He needed her wetness, her heat. He pushed her back until she sat on the bed. He removed her boots and socks and shimmied her jeans and panties down her shapely legs.

"Spread your legs, darlin'," he said, his voice nearly unrecognizable.

She obeyed, and he stood, tantalized. She was truly beautiful, pink and swollen and glistening.

He positioned himself in front of that treasure and darted his tongue out to taste her.

She jolted. "Oh my God."

"Mmm, baby, you taste so good." He swirled his tongue through her moist folds. Just like the rest of her—tangy, sweet, and smoky so perfectly combined. How long had it been since he'd tasted a woman? Far too long. And never had he tasted a woman so delicious, so satisfying.

She writhed beneath him, fisted her hands in his long hair, pulling it loose from its ponytail. "God, yes, Rafe. Lick me. So good."

She ground into his mouth, and her sex pulsed against his face. She was going to come. This quickly, she was coming. He felt like a horny teenager. He couldn't wait to sink himself into that moist heat.

But right now, he'd give her an orgasm. He thrust two fingers into her—her suction grabbed him—and her hips rose. As he tongued her clit, he circled his fingers and found the spot that sent her over the edge.

"Yes, yes!" She moved her hips to his rhythm.

She pulsed against his lips and fingers, and a smooth veil of moisture cascaded over his hand like a soft blanket.

Damn, she's a squirter.

He'd had his share of experience, but he'd never been with a woman who squirted. He'd always considered the g-spot orgasm to be a myth.

He found, suddenly, that he was thrilled beyond words.

He continued to lick her while he fumbled with his own pants and kicked off his boots. Condom? His wallet. "I'll be right back, baby," he said.

Angie was still writhing, coming down from her orgasm. Rafe found the condom and quickly sheathed himself.

And thrust into her.

Sweet Jesus, she's tight. So tight and so slick. She enveloped him in moist heat. He pushed into her, out, and in again.

Her words swirled around him and bathed him in contentment. The sound of his name, the endearments, how much pleasure he was giving her—all met his ears and took away the solitude that had been his life for too long.

Far too long.

He thrust and he thrust, harder and faster, until he hit the precipice and spilled into her.

So close. So wonderful. He didn't want to withdraw.

When he finally regained his senses, he realized he hadn't even taken his shirt off. He'd missed the sensation of those lovely breasts against his chest. He smiled. There was always next time.

And there would definitely be a next time.

CHAPTER FIVE

"When are you going to stop worrying about me and settle down?"

Rafe adjusted his father's humidifier. Damn thing wasn't working right again. He'd have to get a new one at the pharmacy. At least they weren't very expensive.

"I'm not even close to settling down, Dad. How about you? Ma's been gone a couple years. You're still a good-lookin' man. There's plenty of eligible ladies around here."

"None who want a man who lives in a trailer." He smiled. "Besides, I'm not lonely."

"Stop selling yourself short. And I don't believe you're not lonely. Where is Lilia, anyway?"

"She went into town on errands." He coughed. "You and your brother need to stop frettin' over me."

"Has Tom been by?"

"Just this morning. Said he got a job tendin' bar over at the Bullfrog a couple nights a week. A job he says you turned down."

"Yeah, turns out I got a better way to earn some extra cash."

"Oh?"

"I'm giving riding lessons."

Jack Grayhawk nodded. "You're certainly qualified. No one understands horses like you do. You always amazed me."

Rafe laughed. "You taught me everything I know. Tom

too. You're the best."

"Not anymore, with my health the way it is."

"You're healthy as a horse, Dad. You just need a change of climate. The four seasons don't agree with you. You need warm dry air all year long, and you'll be good as new. Doc says so."

Jack raked his fingers through his gray hair. "Tell me about these riding lessons."

"You're changing the subject."

"Damn right, I am. You and your brother are so convinced I'm lonely. I'm absolutely fine here with Lilia. So what gives with the lessons?"

"I'm teaching Angelina Bay. She's Catie's sister-in-law."

"Princess? Wow."

Rafe shot his eyebrows up. "Princess? She's thirty-two years old."

"Yeah, but that's what her father called her, I think. Her mother, Maria—man, she's a pretty one."

So was her daughter, though he wasn't going to get into that with his father. "How do you know the lot of them?"

"I did some construction for them a few years ago, before my accident." He stared wistfully into space. "I always got the feeling Mia—that's what her husband called her, and it seemed to fit—wasn't quite as happy as she should be. Like something was missing."

Strange. What could his father be talking about? "What do you mean?"

"Not sure I know. She's a beauty. Dark hair, dark eyes. Her other two were gone away to school. The little one somewhere in Europe, and the boy in Denver at law school, but Angie was around. A gorgeous girl."

Well, some things hadn't changed at all. Angie was still gorgeous. And a squirter. Sheesh, he still couldn't get over that one. Course he wouldn't mention that particular detail to his father.

"Angelina's still a beauty."

"Oh, no doubt. I see her on occasion when I'm picking stuff up in town. Course she doesn't know me from Adam. Mia remembers me though, always speaks when she sees me. Such a sweet woman. Reminds me of your mother."

Angie's mother reminded Jack of Rafe's mother? The apple definitely fell far from the tree then. Angie wasn't anything like his mother. Spoiled rotten, Angie was. Goddess-like body and beautiful face, maybe, but definitely spoiled rotten.

His father's dark eyes looked misty. His mother had been gone for nearly three years now, but Jack still missed her. Rafe could tell every time he spoke of her. Yet he insisted he wasn't lonely. Thank goodness Lilia was around to see to Jack's needs. Jack was only fifty, but his asthma kept him pretty housebound during the cold weather. Now, during late summer, he was able to lead a normal life.

"Angelina looks quite a bit like her mother, doesn't she?"

"I haven't met Maria Bay, Dad, so I couldn't say. Angie's eyes aren't brown. They're green as spring grass."

His father chuckled. "Green as spring grass, huh? Not just green. Or not just 'I haven't noticed the color of her eyes.' She got a hold on you, boy?"

A hold on him? Not in this lifetime. She sure was nice for a romp in the hay though. Not that he'd tell his father that. Jack Grayhawk loved the ladies and respected them. He wouldn't appreciate his son romping in the hay with a client.

"Why would you think that? I can't appreciate a woman's eyes without her having a hold on me?"

"You? I highly doubt it." He winked. "I'm kiddin', son. I know you have too high of a work ethic to get involved with someone you're workin' for."

Rafe's cheeks warmed. Hopefully his thoughts weren't apparent. His father was right. He had crossed a line.

Better keep the relationship professional from now on.

Even if she was a squirter.

★ ★ ★

"Good, you're here," Rafe said the next morning.

Angie turned. Had he actually gotten better looking overnight? His shirt was sky blue today, and its contrast with his dark skin mesmerized her. His sleeves were rolled up as usual, and his corded forearms glistened.

She'd finished grooming Belle and hoped they'd actually get to ride this morning. Though if they ended up at the hand's house again, she wouldn't have too many complaints.

"Good job," he said. "Belle looks great. Leave her where she is for now and follow me."

"Huh?" She arched her eyebrows. Was he going to take her straight to bed? Worked for her. Her one-morning stand could be a two-morning stand. Who needed to learn to ride a horse anyway?

Well, she did, or she'd be disinherited. For a minute she despised her father for doing this to her.

"I really think I need a lesson today," she said.

"You'll have a lesson. Follow me."

They left the musty barn and walked outside in the crisp

morning air. A lone chair sat on the grass outside.

"Where'd that come from?" Angie asked.

"I put it there. Come here and sit."

"Huh?" she said again.

"You heard me. Sit."

"Uh...okay." She sat.

"Bend your elbows, as if you're holding reins."

She complied.

"Now, push your elbows down. You want to be sitting deep."

"Not sure I understand."

He leaned down and placed one hand on each of her forearms. Her skin tingled. He pushed gently, causing her upper arms and shoulders to tense slightly.

"Relax," he said. "Feel your bottom on the chair. Become aware of where each part of your bottom is touching the chair."

This was going to teach her to ride a horse? His hands were on her, though. That was a good thing.

"Yesterday I actually got on Belle, remember?"

"Yesterday you slid off Belle, remember?"

True enough. "So this is some newfangled teaching method for today?"

"I wouldn't say it's newfangled. I wouldn't even say it's mine. Let's just say I did a little research. You'll have to trust me."

Her father was paying one hundred dollars an hour for this? So far she'd learned to groom a horse and sit on a chair.

"Now," Rafe continued, "put your hands under your bottom."

She'd rather he put his hands under her bottom, but okay. She did so.

"Can you feel the bones in your butt?"

"Um, yeah."

"Now shift your weight slightly to the left."

She leaned to the left and shifted her weight.

"Try to do it without leaning."

She concentrated on bearing down on her left butt cheek. Felt strange.

"Good," he said. "Can you feel your weight much more on your left hand than your right?"

She nodded.

"Switch to the right now. Remember, don't lean."

Rafe moved behind her and placed one hand on each of her shoulders. Tingles again. With belly flutters this time.

"You're leaning," he said. "You did better on the left, probably because you're left-handed. I'm going to hold you in place till you can do it without leaning."

His hands on me? She shuddered. *I may never learn to do it without leaning.*

She continued to shift her weight from one side of her butt to the other, and gradually Rafe decreased the pressure on her shoulders until he pronounced her ready.

"I'm going to let you use the bit on Belle the first few times, but reins cause horses a lot of pain. I don't like to use them at all."

"But that's how I rode before, with reins."

"I figured as much. So I'm not going to teach you to ride without reins. We'll still use them, but we won't use the bit once you can control the horse with your legs. Belle will thank you for it."

Angie stood, her bottom numb. She rubbed her butt cheeks. "Can we try it now?"

Rafe smiled. *God, his lips are so kissable.*

"Nope. Our hour's up, honey."

"Well...I didn't get the whole hour yesterday."

"Which is why I'm not charging you for yesterday. I do an honest day's work or I don't get paid. That's my philosophy."

Fine enough. Now he'll kiss me and we'll go to bed for another amazing romp. She closed her eyes in expectation.

Nothing happened.

She opened her eyes to see him tip his hat and walk toward the barn with a cheery "see you tomorrow."

He left her with hard nipples and a breathless sigh.

Damn.

★ ★ ★

Jefferson Bay studied the document in front of him. He was no lawyer, but the language seemed clear enough. His grandfather had been one big male chauvinist pig. And that sad fact was going to work in Jeff's favor.

His big brother, Wayne, was dying. According to a PI Jeff had hired, Wayne had an inoperable brain tumor that was growing in size every day, and his heart was weak. He needed a quadruple bypass, but the docs were afraid he wouldn't survive the surgery. Basically, he'd been sent home to die.

He was a ticking time bomb that could explode at any time. Damn shame, wasn't it? Wayne, Grandpa's pride and joy, would die, and Jeff would finally be vindicated.

He smiled to himself and downed a shot of Jack Daniels. The whiskey burned and soothed his throat simultaneously. He'd missed ol' Jack most of all while he'd been locked up.

Well, almost most of all. He'd missed something—

someone—else more. No matter how hard he tried, he couldn't shake that woman from his heart.

Didn't matter though. He'd learned to live without her long ago, despite his searing need. He'd continue to do so.

He poured himself another shot.

Yeah, life would be good again.

CHAPTER SIX

There she stood again, those pink-as-a-rose hands on those round hips, looking as indignant as ever. Her emerald eyes glared at him.

"You have some explaining to do, Mr. Grayhawk."

"I do?"

"You certainly do."

"And just what would that be about?"

"We were"—Angie cleared her throat—"*intimate* the other day."

Why was she so damn gorgeous? She wore her hair down today, and those silky waves tumbled over her bare shoulders clad in nothing but a pink tank top. He wanted to bury his nose in those tresses and inhale.

Rafe nodded. "I remember. I was there."

"We haven't talked about it."

"So?" What was it with women and talking?

He sighed. He did owe her an explanation. He had overstepped his boundaries with her twice, and it wasn't going to happen again.

"So? That's all you have to say?"

His turn to clear his throat. "No. I do need to say something." He paused. "I'm sorry."

Her lips curled into a snarl. "Sorry?"

Clearly not what she thought she'd hear.

"Yes, I'm very sorry, Angelina. I won't deny that I'm

attracted to you, but I'm a professional, and I violated my work ethic. If you want to find another riding instructor, I understand."

"Find another instructor? Are you serious?" She paced back and forth. "Chad handpicked you for my father. He's insisting I learn to ride, and so far all I've learned is how to clench my butt in a chair."

And what a finely-shaped butt it was. He itched to caress the contours of that perfect feature.

"You've learned how to sit on a horse. You'll see the value of that tomorrow when we have our lesson."

"What if—" She stopped abruptly.

"What if what?"

"Oh never mind!" She stormed off.

He shook his head. Now what? She didn't actually want to continue their liaison, did she? They were dynamite together, no doubt, but she'd made it crystal clear that she considered him beneath her socially. Wait until she found out he'd grown up in a trailer park and his father still lived there.

How beautiful she'd been when she came for him. Whispered his name as he held her afterward. He stiffened. How she affected him physically. Even emotionally on some level. He sighed. If only things were different, maybe they'd have a chance.

But he could never marry, and a girl like Angie deserved marriage and a family. Even a spoiled brat deserved more than he could offer.

He checked his watch. Almost quitting time. Thank God. He needed a drink.

★ ★ ★

"Catie!" Angie waltzed right into her sister's house. "Where are you?"

"In here," her sister called from the kitchen.

Angie walked to the back of the house and found her sister at the table. "Hi, Cheryl," she said to the cook.

"Hi, Miss Angie," Cheryl said without turning around.

"Smells great."

"Lasagna in the oven," Catie said. "One of Chad's favorites."

"Where is Chad? I need to talk to him."

"He'll be in soon. You want to stay for dinner?"

Angie nodded and sat down. "Thanks. I'd love to if you don't mind. I've been following Harper around on the ranch all day and I'm starved."

"You don't look like you've been ranching all day."

"I went home and showered. Harp yelled at me for knocking off early, but I told him to fuck off."

Catie laughed. "You told Harper to fuck off? That's great, Ang. Bet that went over like a ton of bricks."

"Yeah, he wasn't too pleased, but I don't rightly care. I'm exhausted."

"What are you doing over here then?"

"Came over to talk to Rafe."

"Yeah? How are the lessons going?"

"Great. So far I've learned how to sit in a chair."

Catie laughed again. "So he's teaching you to ride without reins? Good for him. That's what's best for the horse."

"It's not how you learned."

"No, not at first, but I eventually learned to use very little rein. I still keep the reins handy, just in case, but I don't rely on them at all."

Angie rolled her eyes. "Well, goodie for you."

"If you came over here to be a bitch, you can leave," Catie said.

Angie sighed. "I'm sorry. I came to speak to Chad, actually. It's just been a rough day."

"Yes, I know. Rough day of ranch work. Stuff Harp and I have been doing for years."

"I know, I know. God, am I really that awful?"

"You're spoiled, no doubt."

"That's what Amber said too."

"Amber's right."

"What happened to me? Why not you? Why not Harp?"

"Harp's a boy, and Daddy got him started with work at a young age, I guess. As for me, I came along so much later and I loved horses and the ranch so much, it just naturally fit my personality."

"I suppose."

"Well, that's my story and I'm sticking to it. You're just a different kind of girl than I was, Ang. It's okay."

"It's Daddy's fault, really. Why didn't he insist I learn all this stuff earlier? Did you know he's threatened to cut me out of the will if I don't learn about ranching?"

Catie's eyes widened. "Really? No, I didn't know. But Angie, you can't seriously blame Dad for you not learning this stuff."

"Why not?"

"Because it's not his fault. You've been hanging around here since you got out of college. That was ten years ago, for God's sake."

"I've done stuff."

"Preparing me to be rodeo queen doesn't count."

"I've prepared a contestant every year, I'll have you kn○ Some of them even paid me."

"Dad pays for your living expenses and everything, does○ he?"

She warmed. Surely her cheeks were turning crimson.

"You haven't worked either. You went to school, and the○ you married Chad."

"If you think I don't work around here, you're crazy. I do a load of work every day. I'm up with the birds taking care of horses and taking care of this house."

Angie rolled her eyes toward Cheryl. "You have a cook, for goodness' sake."

"It just so happens that my cooking stinks. That doesn't mean I don't pull my weight around here."

She'd hit a nerve with her sister, clearly. "Where can Chad be?"

"He'll be in. What did you want to talk to him about anyway?"

Easy. She wanted to tell him that his ranch hand, Mr. Rafe Grayhawk, had behaved unprofessionally toward her and she wanted to have him fired. Chad would do it for her, wouldn't he? If not for her, for Catie. He'd lose his job, and she'd be the catalyst. No one treated Angelina Bay the way Rafe had treated her. Not without consequences, that was for sure.

An image flashed in her mind—the horrified look on Judy Williamson's face when she'd botched Angie's color and Angie had threatened to run her out of business. Judy's cheeks had reddened, and fear had washed over her eyes.

Angie'd been horrible that day. An emotion tugged at

sadness, not quite guilt.

w.   first time, she felt ashamed of her behavior.
          how she'd treated Judy that day. Ashamed of what
't   here to do.

          it her lip. She could have Rafe fired in a minute, but
       what she really wanted? If Rafe left, who would teach
     de? If Rafe left, how would he earn a living?

    id if Rafe left, she'd never see him again.

   hat thought niggled at her, bit at her like a pesky fruit fly.
   He'd taken her to paradise and back. If he were gone, she'd
  er experience that ecstasy again.

   No, he needed to stay put. For his own good and for hers.

   His ethics still proved problematic. That'd be a challenge.
   ourse Angelina Bay could seduce an ethical ranch hand sure
  enough. She'd already done it.

She hadn't yet had her fill of Rafe Grayhawk. One-morning stand be damned! She'd have as many morning stands as she wanted before she—and she alone—decided it was over.

"Hey, sugar." Chad McCray sauntered in. "How long till dinner? I need a shower somethin' awful."

Angie wrinkled her nose at the aroma of dirt and steer. He sure did need a shower.

Cheryl turned from the counter. "About fifteen minutes, Mr. Chad."

"That's plenty of time," Catie said. "Go ahead and wash up. Angie's staying for dinner. She wants to talk to you."

"Oh yeah? What's up, Ang?"

Angie cleared her throat. "It's nothing important. Nothing I can't handle alone, actually. Let's just have a nice dinner."

"Sounds great to me," Chad said. "See you in a few." He

headed upstairs.

"Spill it," Catie said. "What's going on?"

"Nothing, I promise. But before Chad comes down, I want to know every single thing you can tell me about Rafe Grayhawk."

★ ★ ★

Angie still cringed. Every hair on her body stood upright.

Rafe Grayhawk was twenty-five years old. Seven years her junior! And he'd grown up in the trailer park on the south side of town. The south side, a step below the west side, which was the bad part of town.

He was descended from the Comanche on his father's side, Irish and Lakota Sioux on his mother's. Nearly a full-blooded Native American. That part hadn't surprised her. He sure as heck looked the part. Put him in a pair of buckskins with a feather in that long black hair and place him atop a pinto and he'd be the picture of a young warrior. He'd steal the heart of every girl in the State of Colorado.

His mother had passed away about three years ago, though Catie didn't know how. His father still lived in the family trailer in Echo Gardens, the trailer park on the south side. A Mexican woman named Lilia lived with him and kept house. She worked part time for Jason McCourt, a realtor in town. Rafe's father had retired from construction work on disability due to a hip injury, and he had chronic asthma and had a hard time with Colorado winters. Rafe had a brother, Tom, about two years older and divorced. He worked as a mechanic for Joe Bradley in town. He and Rafe shared the small two bedroom apartment above Annie McCray's vet office. Rafe, to Catie's knowledge, had never been married.

No wonder Angie had never seen hide nor hair of Rafe or his brother. She and Harper were too old to have known them in high school, and Catie, at nearly twenty-two, too young.

When Chad came down to dinner, Angie's appetite had waned. She excused herself and left. She pondered all Catie had told her as she drove to her house on her father's property.

Had she not been intimate with the man, she'd have called him trailer trash. It was a term she used often, though less since she'd stopped hanging around with Dallas McCray's ex-wife, Chelsea. That bitch had been a bad seed, no doubt. A few years ago, she'd poisoned Dallas's cattle. And all that after he'd given her a seven figure settlement! Why she hadn't taken the money and run, Angie had no idea.

She sighed. Chelsea had been fun to shop with for sure, but the woman possessed no real depth.

But did Angie? Was she headed that route herself? She'd certainly never poison anyone's livestock.

Trailer trash?

Rafe?

He spoke well. She'd only heard him say "ain't" once, though that meant nothing. The McCray boys habitually used that word, and they were all intelligent and highly educated.

Rafe and Tom had both finished high school but hadn't gone to college. No doubt their parents hadn't been able to afford higher education. They lived in a trailer, after all.

So she wouldn't marry the guy. He was a ranch hand, for goodness' sake. That didn't mean they couldn't screw each other's brains out. Truth be told, he was better in the sack than any she'd had, including Zach McCray.

He'd shown her a passion, an intensity, that no other man

had. And though it'd been five years since she'd had any, she'd had plenty in her younger days for comparison.

But a trailer? Angie couldn't quite wrap her mind around the concept.

Abruptly, she stopped her car and turned around. The evening was sunny and warm. The sun hovered right above the mountains, magenta clouds surrounding it. A beautiful sunset was on the horizon. Why not take a drive?

And why not check out Echo Gardens trailer park?

CHAPTER SEVEN

"You feelin' up to a drink at the Bullfrog?" Rafe asked his father. "Tom told me he's working tonight."

The door of the trailer jiggled and in walked Lilia. "Hi, Rafe," she said in her Mexican accent. "You staying for dinner?"

"Don't mind if I do," Rafe said, "and after that, I'm takin' Dad for a drink. You want to join us?"

She shook her head. "You two go ahead. I'm beat. I'm going to warm up some tamales and then hit the sack."

"Homemade tamales?"

"There's no other kind." She smiled.

Lilia was a pretty woman. Not beautiful, but pleasantly pretty with an attractive curvy figure. Her olive skin and dark eyes provided a nice contrast to the pastel hues she always wore. She was thirty-five now. Thirty-five and still happy to be keeping house for Jack.

Rafe said a silent prayer of thanks for her. She could easily go out on her own and find better paying work than answering phones for Jake McCourt. He and Tom had made it abundantly clear that she owed no debt to either them or their father. Yet still she stayed in the trailer park, making sure Jack was fed and his home clean.

After a dinner of Lilia's delicious tamales, Rafe dragged his father out of the house to the Bullfrog for a beer. Jack was still a nice-looking man, and there was no reason he shouldn't get out when he could. Rafe worried about him, how he'd never seemed to quite get over his wife's death. The wistful looks he got when her name was mentioned, or when he looked at Lilia, no doubt imagining Finola in her place. How he rarely left the trailer.

"Come on, old man," he said to his father as he parked in back of the bar. "Time to have a little fun."

★ ★ ★

Not a bad little place, really. So it was a trailer park. The children running around for the most part looked clean and well-fed. What had she been thinking? That trailer trash didn't take care of their children? Some of the men and women sitting outside were overweight, but all classes had overweight people. And yes, some of them were sitting on plastic lawn furniture. So what? It was inexpensive seating from Walmart. Big deal.

Which one was Rafe's? No way to know, really. They all looked alike. Cracker boxes painted different shades of gray and green. Nope, there was a beige one. Some of them needed exterior work, but quite a few of them were amazingly well kept. How had she been so wrong about people? She'd always assumed lower income people took no pride in their appearances or their homes.

Rafe certainly did. He took pride in his work and in himself. He even spoke better than a lot of the educated people she knew. Truth be told, he hadn't been out of her mind since she'd first laid eyes on him. He was always there, niggling at her. The sweet memory of their kisses, their lovemaking.

Her heart quickened. What was she saying? She was not falling love with the man. She hardly knew him. He was way too young. She was no cougar. And even though she now knew he was much more than she'd first thought, they still had nothing in common.

Nothing at all.

Except dynamite chemistry in the bedroom. They couldn't build a relationship on that.

She sighed. Quickly she texted Amber and arranged to meet her at the Bullfrog for a drink. She wanted to drown her sorrows.

She drove back into town, parked her car, and headed into the bar. Amber had arrived and already ordered their first round. A cosmo for her and a dry martini for Angie. She was laughing with a new bartender.

A new bartender who looked oddly like Rafe.

Angie walked toward them and saw it couldn't possibly be Rafe. His hair was much shorter and had a little wave to it. It brushed his broad shoulders. The skin color, eyes, and facial characteristics were dead on, though.

"Hey there," Amber said. "Meet Tom, the new bartender. And you'll never guess whose brother he is."

"Rafe Grayhawk's," Angie returned.

Tom let out a laugh. "Yeah, the resemblance is pretty uncanny. So you're Angie."

"Born and bred." She held out her hand. He had a firm handshake like his brother. Funny, her skin didn't tingle at the touch. He was every bit as handsome as Rafe.

What was going on?

"Thanks for getting the drinks," she said to Amber. "Next round's on me." The next round would be Amber's last. Her friend never drank more than two cosmopolitans. Said she'd had some bad times with alcohol in her past. Someday Angie'd get the scoop on that.

But not today. Today was for her to confide in her friend about Rafe.

Course she could hardly do that with his brother standing right there. She sighed and turned to look down the counter at the rest of the bar.

Her heart sped up.

Rafe.

Not all men could pull off a bright red shirt, but he surely could. It was perfect with his dark skin and black hair. And oh, his hair. He wore it loose tonight. She'd never seen it that way before. Straight, black as night, and longer than her own. It flowed down his back and over his shoulders like an ebony curtain.

Whoever said long hair was not masculine had never set eyes on Rafe Grayhawk.

He sat the very end of the bar with an older gentleman sporting the same dark skin and black eyes. His father?

She took three long gulps of her drink. There was one way to find out. She excused herself to Amber and walked toward Rafe. A tequila sunrise sat in front of him. A beer in front of the other man.

"Hello," she said.

He looked up. "Hi there. What are you doing here?"

"Same as you, I'd say. Having a drink." She gave him what she hoped was a coy smile. "Who's your friend?"

The older man's eyes lit up like Christmas. "Aren't you kind? I'm Jack Grayhawk. Rafe's father."

"Dad, this is Angelina Bay," Rafe said.

"Yes, I know. I did some work at your ranch some years back. Nice to see you."

The older man held out his hand and Angie took it. Same great looks as his sons, same warm grip.

No sparks.

As an experiment, she lightly touched Rafe's forearm. A jolt shot through her.

Yep. Sparks.

Out of nowhere, she said, "Would you like to dance with me, Rafe?"

Rafe's eyebrows shot up. Silence.

Jack Grayhawk cleared his throat. "Son, I thought I'd taught you this a long time ago. When a beautiful young lady asks you to dance, you say yes."

Did Rafe's cheeks actually redden just a little?

Angie smiled. "Your father's right. Could I have the pleasure?"

Rafe stood, but said nothing. Black jeans curved over that beautiful backside. Angie's breath caught.

The DJ started a new song. A slow one. Was that good or bad? Angie couldn't decide. She'd be able to touch him, but he might think she'd talked to the DJ ahead of time.

He didn't seem too daunted though. He took her hand— *yep, sparks*—and led her to the floor. He pulled her against his body and started swaying to the melody.

Angie closed her eyes and breathed against his neck. He smelled the same, maybe a bit cleaner, but still outdoors and slightly coconut. Strands of hair tickled her cheeks. Perfect.

The perfect dance.

Her nipples tightened against his chest until she was certain he'd feel them poking him. She didn't care Let him know how turned on she was, what he did to her. If he didn't know by now, he was clueless anyway.

She inhaled again, savoring his masculine scent, his manly chest, his coconut hair. Yes, it was his hair. Rafe used coconut shampoo. For some reason, that fact turned her on even more.

Her nipples ached. Ached for his kisses, his tongue, his teeth. Her sex pulsed between her legs in dreamy time with the music. Mmm, how his lips had melted her flesh as he pleasured her, stroked her to orgasm with his fingers and tongue.

She was wet now. The moisture was apparent as she moved against him.

If only she could lean upward, take his lips with her own, kiss him with the passion and desire pent within her. Those beautiful pink lips. Talented lips. Lips like none she'd ever kissed before.

Rafe's lips.

Rafe's body.

Rafe's hard cock pressed into her belly.

She smiled against his red shirt.

He wanted her just as much.

She pressed into his crotch. He pulsed against her. God, she wanted him. Wanted him to fill her—fill that aching empty place inside her body. Inside her soul.

She leaned upward and pressed her lips to his.

Sweet, sweet kiss. He opened for her. Ran his tongue across first her upper lip and then her lower before easing it into her mouth. The citrusy tang of his drink mingled with the juniper and olive of her martini. Different. Different and delicious.

Rafe.

His arms tightened around her and he ground his hardness against her. Their kiss continued, aggressive and timeless. Angie no longer cared who saw her, who was around her. Were there others on the dance floor? Or were she and Rafe alone? Were they still in the bar, or were they holding each other outside, under the stars?

She groaned into his mouth, took all she could from him and gave. Yes, she gave. Gave the kiss of a lifetime to this man who made her crazy. So crazy.

One hand wandered downward, and she began to rub her palm against the bulge in his jeans.

She felt, more than heard, his groan.

They danced, they swayed, they kissed. One.

They were one.

"Time to cut in."

Amber's voice cut into her fantasy. A shadow jerked her from Rafe.

"What in God's name are you two doing?" Amber quickly inserted herself between them and continued the dance with Rafe at a reasonable distance. "Go outside and hose yourself down."

Angie shook her head to clear it. What had she been thinking? What had they both been thinking? She'd been ready to rip her shirt off so she could feel Rafe's silky tongue on her hard nipples. Had Amber not intervened, she might have.

She headed out the back way to the parking lot. The crisp night air wasn't cool, but at least she could breathe. A few minutes later, Amber appeared.

"Tom and I managed to keep their father's attention away from you two, thank God. What were you thinking?"

Angie stared into space. "I don't know. I honestly don't know."

"Well, he was obviously thinking the same thing." Amber let out a huge breath. "I told him Tom said it was time to get his dad home. After he came back to earth, he agreed and apologized all over the place."

"So you didn't have a whole dance?"

"Angie, I had no desire to have a dance with your man."

Her man? The words trickled over her like warm honey.

"I was just trying to keep you two from getting arrested. You were making quite a spectacle. If I hadn't stopped you, you'd have been having sex on the floor of the Bullfrog."

"I think I have a little more self-control than that."

"Not from where I was standing. If you don't believe me, ask Tom. It was his idea for me to cut in."

Angie jolted back to reality. God. Rafe's brother. And Rafe's father. "His dad didn't see us, did he?"

"Weren't you listening before? Tom kept him occupied. I don't think he noticed."

Angie breathed a sigh of relief. Her body felt like lead. "Amber, I think I'm going to head on home. I'm feeling a little... odd."

"I'm not surprised."

"What do I owe you?"

"Nothing. Just get the drinks next time."

"Thanks, you're a gem. See you later." She walked to her car, her body still throbbing. Mr. Ace would be on call tonight.

CHAPTER EIGHT

"I want to apologize—"

Angie stopped Rafe's words. "No need. It was my fault. I kissed you."

"I certainly didn't stop you."

"Fine. We were both at fault. I'm just glad Amber and Tom kept their heads." She forced a smile. "So am I going to actually get on Belle today?"

"Yes." He smiled back.

Dear God, he is gorgeous. Today he wore work jeans and a beige shirt, his hair in the low ponytail, and a bandana, this time red, tied on as a do-rag under his cowboy hat. How could a simple ranch hand in such simple clothing be so beautiful?

Because he wasn't a simple ranch hand. She'd been blind for too long. He came from a humble background, but that didn't matter. His work ethic was strong, so unlike her own. He made her want to change. He made her want to be a better person. A better person like him. His real beauty, though strong on the outside, resided inside him.

He was perfect.

"Here, let me help you."

She tingled as his hand brushed against her. In a few seconds, she had mounted.

"I want you to turn your body to the left. Look at a point at, say, nine o'clock."

She turned her head.

"No. Your whole body, not just your head. Swivel your shoulders. Now what's happening to your seat and legs?"

"I don't know."

"Close your eyes and do it again. Swivel to the left. Pay attention to what your body is doing. You need to know your body as well as your horse does, and vice versa."

She sighed and shut her eyes tight.

"Relax."

"Okay, okay." She swiveled to the left. "My left leg is going forward a bit, my right leg backward."

"What's happening to your butt?"

"I guess I've got more weight on the right side. Well, just more pressure, maybe."

"Good. Belle is going to move away from the pressure, so she'll move to the left. You ready?"

"I guess so." She felt good being on a horse again. It had been years, a decade maybe, since she'd ridden, and then she'd depended solely on reins.

"Get her walking and circle to the left when I tell you."

Angie clicked her tongue, and to her surprise, Belle started walking. Her father had chosen a well-trained horse. Of course he had. Wayne Bay never did anything halfway.

Including spoiling his daughter.

She freed that thought from her mind. This moment was for her and Belle. She didn't want to use a crop or whip to start her, and she knew Rafe would hate that too.

"Good job. Now we're going to circle to the left. Go ahead and swivel and look to nine o'clock."

Belle didn't move.

"Why isn't it working?"

"She's probably been mouth trained. Lift your rein just

slightly."

It worked! Belle veered to the left.

"We're going to keep at this till she responds without the rein."

About a half hour later, Angie and Belle were circling to the right and the left without any reins. Rafe's smile told her he was pleased.

"Great job today, Angelina."

Was he intentionally creating distance? "We've been through this. I wish you'd call me Angie."

"I don't know. Angelina fits you better."

"But it sounds so... I don't know." Too classy? Is that what she was going to say? Too what? She wasn't sure. All she knew was that it was important to her that Rafe call her Angie.

"Please?" She used the word and the batting eyes that always worked on her daddy. Till now, of course.

To her astonishment, it worked.

"All right...Angie. Great work today. I hate to tell you this, but you're going to be saddle sore, so I recommend a hot bath tonight. You go on home. I'll take care of Belle today. See you tomorrow." He took Belle's reins and turned toward the barn.

"But—"

He turned back to face her.

What had she wanted to say? *Don't leave? Kiss me again? Take me to bed? I think I might be falling for you?*

While he clearly enjoyed her physically, he obviously had no interest in her in any other way. Probably thought she was a horny spoiled brat who was too old for him anyway.

Which, of course, was all true.

She stood with her mouth agape, most likely looking like an idiot, when her cell phone rang.

Saved by the bell. Literally.

"Hi, Mama," she said into the phone.

"Angie." Her mother's voice was low and hollow. "Come home right away. It's Daddy."

* * *

"Why didn't you tell us about this?" Angie demanded.

Maria Bay sat quietly in the hospital waiting area. "Please don't make a scene, Angie. It was your father's wish not to burden you kids."

"Burden us?" Catie's pretty face reddened. "He's our father!"

"It wasn't my choice, Caitlyn." Maria shook her head. "It was his. I wanted to tell you."

"But if we'd known, we could have—" Angie stopped midsentence. Could have what? Treated him more kindly? Spent more time with him? Not thrown a fit about riding lessons and learning to ranch? She should have been doing all that anyway.

She was Daddy's girl. Daddy's princess. How could she have been so shallow? How could she have considered her father's life work so unimportant? She plunked down next to her mother, buried her face in her hands, and wept.

Shaking hands rubbed her back lightly. "Angie, he might pull through."

Angie turned and looked up into her mother's sunken eyes. "Might? You heard what the doctor said. They wouldn't do the heart surgery because they were afraid he wouldn't live through it. Now with the heart attack, they have no choice. So he's in worse condition, and you think he'll pull through? And if he does, the brain tumor will kill him within a month anyway."

Her mother simply stared.

Harper sat down on her other side. "Lay off her, Angie. This is the toughest on her."

"Harper's right," Catie said.

"You never even loved him," Angie went on. "You married him because you were pregnant with me. He deserved to be loved."

"So did Mom, Ang," Catie said.

"We did love each other." Maria wiped her eyes. "We grew to love each other very much. We just weren't *in* love."

"You denied him being in love?" Angie wrung her hands. "How could you?"

"I didn't deny him anything. It was his decision to stay with me. After you came along, there was no way he would have left. He adored you, Angelina. You were the light of his eye. His princess."

Just what she didn't need to hear at this moment. Angie sniffed, taking the tissue Catie handed her. She'd taken her father for granted for too long. Well, no longer. If he got through this, she'd spend way more time with him. She'd learn everything in the world there was to know about ranching, and she'd make him proud.

"He was always proud of you," her mother said softly, as though reading her mind. "All three of you."

"We know that, Ma," Harper said. "And he loved you too."

"I know he did. We both sacrificed passion for you children, but that was our choice." She looked at Angie. "And it was just as much his choice as mine."

Angie looked up at the painting in the waiting area—all red with black splotches. She'd first seen the painting when she sat in this very room during Zach McCray's illness over four years ago. That was the day she'd given up on Zach forever. He'd found true love with Dusty, now his wife. He'd never loved Angie the way he loved Dusty, if at all.

Truth be told, Angie hadn't loved Zach like that either. They'd been good together, but she never felt that all-consuming fire, that crazy passion, that "can't get you out of my mind for a minute" frenzy. She'd never felt it for Zach or anyone, so how could she describe it now?

Rafe.

She was in love with Rafe.

Damn it all to hell.

"Mrs. Bay?"

Angie looked up. The doctor, a gray-haired woman, removed her surgical mask. "He's in ICU. He made it, but I can't lie to you. Every minute is precious right now."

"Can I sit with him?"

"Yes, but only you for now."

"You kids go on home," Maria said. "There's nothing you can do here."

"Are you crazy? We can't leave," Harper said.

"You need to be at the ranch, Harp. You know he'd want that. And Catie, you're in a delicate condition. Go home. Angie, you look terrible. Go home and get some rest."

"It's over an hour drive home," Angie said. "What if something happens?"

"You all have cells. I'll call you."

"We should see him," Harper said.

"All right," the doctor said. "But only for a minute or two. Then listen to your mother. She's right. Go home."

★ ★ ★

If only she'd listened to her mother and gone home. The image of her father in a hospital gown, unconscious, tubes sticking out of his body, haunted her. Why hadn't she noticed how much weight he'd lost? Harper had mentioned it in passing a couple weeks ago, but she'd pooh-poohed him and said Daddy was fine.

And why hadn't it occurred to her to question why he was suddenly so interested in her learning the ranching business? She'd assumed he was just being a belligerent old man.

She truly was shallow.

No longer. Now she'd live a meaningful life and make her daddy proud. She'd be the best damn rancher in the whole state of Colorado, and she'd learn to ride as well or better than Catie.

And despite what her father had done, she'd never settle for anything less than true, unbridled, passionate love.

She drove, staring ahead, not paying much attention to traffic, which was light, luckily.

She didn't want to go home. Didn't want to be alone. Didn't want to talk to anyone, but still didn't want the isolated loneliness of her own home. She wanted strong arms, warm words.

Instead of turning off the main road to get to her house on the ranch, she drove through town. Stopped right in front of the vet's office and parked in back. Walked up the stairs to the apartment where Rafe lived. Hoping Tom was working tonight, she knocked.

The door opened, and a shirtless Rafe appeared.

Bronze hairless chest, dark brown nipples. She couldn't

help herself.

She fell into his arms, sobbing.

CHAPTER NINE

"Angie? What is it?"

His low voice soothed her, its honey tone a warm blanket for her fatigued brain.

"Take me to bed, Rafe."

He picked her up—how wonderful his arms felt around her—and carried her across the tiny living area to a bedroom. Gently he laid her down on a rumpled bed. "What's the matter, baby?"

Angie couldn't talk about it. Didn't want to. Not yet. "Please make love to me."

He hovered over her, placed his hand on one side of her face with the gentlest, almost reverent, touch. "Tell me."

"Please," she said again, her voice but a hoarse whisper now. .

His lips met hers, softly at first, just small kisses around the outside of her mouth. She parted her lips and his tongue swept in gently. They kissed slowly, passionately, their tongues intertwining and their lips sliding. He pushed his hardness into her as they kissed, ground against her.

Her weakened body melted into the soft coverlet. If only she could become one with the bed, the room...with Rafe. Drown her sorrows in this magnificent man. What a soothing salve for the horror that was today.

But Rafe deserved better. She deserved better.

They both deserved a partner who made love for the

right reason. She could escape with him. And she would. But it would not be merely an escape. It would be an act of passion. An act of love.

Because she loved him.

She was crazy in love with him. She had to tell him. But would he return her love?

The thought that he might not cut into her like a spear. What if he didn't love her back? What if this was only sex to him?

But oh, his kisses. He trailed his lips over her cheeks and neck, and he tongued the outer rim of her ear, her lobe, and then probed inside. She shivered. Her whole body quaked. His lips, his tongue, even the soft whisper of his breath sent blazes rippling over her.

That amazing chest, that long hair falling in an onyx veil around her as he nibbled. *Oh, so amazing, so good...so right.*

"Rafe," she whispered. "Rafe, make love to me."

He slowly unbuttoned her blouse, unclasped her bra, and removed them both.

"You are so beautiful." His breath swept over her nipples and turned them hard. "I've never seen such a beautiful body, such a beautiful face, such a beautiful woman." He closed his lips over one turgid peak.

"Oh!" She sighed. "Yes, kiss my nipples, Rafe. Please."

"Mmm, any time, baby. So beautiful."

He tugged at the bud, tantalized her whole body. His fingers traveled up to the other breast and circled the other nipple. Flicked it. Pinched it. She spread her legs, urging him to dry grind against her.

He obliged. She raised her hips to meet him, melding that sweet spot into him.

"Baby, I'm so hard for you," he whispered against the swell of her breast. "I want you so much."

"I want you too. Come inside me. Please."

"Mmm, not yet," he teased. "I'm not done tasting you."

He let her nipple go with a soft pop and then worked her belt and zipper. Soon her boots, jeans, and panties were in a heap on the floor and his tongue was between her legs, caressing her wet folds.

She shivered, she writhed. He tugged on her, sucked on her, flicked his tongue in and out of her wet heat. She raised her thighs and hugged his head with them, urging him farther and farther into her depth.

"Rafe, that feels so good. God, I—"

She almost said the three words. Not the time. She let her head drift back into the clouds as he pleasured her.

"You taste great, baby, like fresh peach pie."

His words sent tingles over her skin. His tongue and lips sent her over the edge. She reached forward, grabbed two fistfuls of his hair, and forced his face farther into her heat.

And she soared to the highest peak in Colorado.

As she drifted downward, his face appeared, his chin glistening with her juices.

"Kiss me," he said. "Taste yourself on me."

The most erotic words she'd ever heard. She pulled him to her and kissed him—a hard, possessive kiss that mingled their scents together and seared their mouths in white heat. They made love with their mouths, tangling their tongues, each letting out little groans as they meshed.

Rafe ripped his mouth away. "God, baby, I have to be inside you." He stood and made short work of his jeans and boxers.

He reached into his night table drawer and grabbed a condom.

No.

The words were sharp in Angie's head.

No. Rafe. Only Rafe inside her.

"Please," she said. "No condom. I've been on the pill forever, and I promise I'm clean."

His black eyes widened and a smile crept to his face. "You sure?"

"God, yes. I need you inside me. Only you."

"Oh, baby, I'm clean too, I promise."

He lowered himself and thrust into her.

How complete she felt, how utterly in love. He started slowly, moving his hips in circles as he thrust, and every inch of her channel felt the sensation. The sensation of Rafe. Only Rafe.

Her hands wandered over his sleek bronze shoulders, his strong back. Oh, the feel of him. Could the finest Asian silk rival Rafe's skin? Never.

His pistoning hips grew stronger, his thrusts harder. Soon he was plunging fast and deep, hitting a spot inside her that made her moan and writhe. The spasms started again, and the winds took her away once more.

"Rafe!" she cried. "Harder, Rafe, harder!"

He sank deeper into her, thrust harder in and out. "Oh, baby, I'm coming." His voice was low and guttural. "God, I'm coming."

One last thrust, and he collapsed upon her breasts. Her fingers tangled in his locks, so soft and silky. "Amazing."

Had that come from her?

"God, baby. Yes. Amazing."

Her heart yearned to say the three words it felt. They clogged her throat, itching to get out. But she couldn't. Not yet. Not until she knew he might feel the same way.

"I should go," she whispered, not wanting to at all.

"Mmm, no." He flipped to the other side of the bed and pulled her into his arms. "Stay." He closed his eyes. "Stay with me."

She snuggled into that hard bronze chest. His heart beat softly into her ear.

She stayed.

★ ★ ★

What a fantastic blow job! Rafe woke from the dream to find he hadn't been dreaming at all. Angie's dark head bobbed between his legs, her cherry lips around his hard cock.

God, how good it felt.

How long had it been since a woman had gone down on him? Too damn long, that was for sure. She nibbled along his shaft, kissed the head, and thrust her mouth downward and took all of him.

Sweet heaven. If he died right now, he'd have no regrets.

She continued her soft torture until he grasped her cheeks and looked into her emerald gaze.

"Come to me, baby. Ride me."

She smiled, slithered forward, and sank her tightness down on his arousal.

"That was the best blow job I've ever had, Angie."

She beamed, her eyes half-lidded. "You have a beautiful cock, Rafe."

Beautiful? A cock was beautiful? Maybe it was. She was

sure beautiful down there, all glossy pink and purple folds, slick with peachy juices. Peachy juices that were slathering all over him right now. She moved her hips up and down, her beautiful breasts jiggling against her chest, her dark waves, tousled from sleep, drifting lazily over her milky shoulders. Those cherry lips were parted slightly. How he wished he could tug on them with his teeth.

"Baby, you look so beautiful right now. Come here." He pulled on her arms, lowering her to him. The tips of her nipples brushed his chest. He squirmed. She excited him like no woman ever had.

"Kiss me," he said.

She attacked his mouth. They ravaged each other's lips as she continued to ride him. He bucked underneath her, meeting her thrust for thrust. Her moans turned to panting, and she ground against his pubic bone. She groaned into his mouth, her heat clamping around him. What a turn on! Her orgasm felt almost as good as his own. Soon the spasms started at the base of his shaft and rushed outward, and he spilled into her warmth.

So wonderful. He didn't want to leave the warm glow of her, but she stood and went to the bathroom. In a few minutes she returned and snuggled back into his arms.

"I think I'm going to be late for my lesson this morning." She chuckled into his chest.

"Baby, you're so past late you're not even in the same city." He checked his watch on the nightstand. Seven thirty. "And so am I."

"Don't worry, I'll talk to Chad."

"Are you crazy? I'm not having my girl make excuses for me. I have to get to work."

"But I wanted to talk—"

"I wish I could, Angie, but I have to go. You want to come by here tonight? Tom's working again, I think. I'll cook you dinner."

Her sparkling green eyes lit up. "You'd cook for me?"

"Sure, I'm a great cook. What do you like?"

"Anything but goat cheese."

He laughed. "I think I can handle that." He kissed her lips. "Stay as long as you like. Tom's probably already up and gone. I'll see you back here at six, okay?"

"Okay." She yawned and closed her eyes.

If only he could stay here and look at her all day. Life would be darn good indeed.

★ ★ ★

His girl.

He'd called her his girl.

Angie smiled and wrapped Rafe's covers more snugly around her. Maybe he could love her.

Her cell phone jolted her back to reality. Her mother. God. How had she almost forgotten what had led her here last night?

"Hi, Mom."

"Angie, you need to get back to the hospital. Things aren't looking good."

Her heart dropped to her belly. "I'm on my way."

Should she shower? No. She gathered her clothes, got into them, and raced out the door of Rafe's apartment. She violated the speed limit all the way to Denver. An hour later, she entered the hospital.

Harper and Catie were already there.

"Mama's in with him now," Catie said.

"What happened?"

"His heart's giving out. He's on machines right now." Harper raked his fingers through his tousled brown hair. "He has a medical power of attorney. He doesn't want to live like this."

Tears welled in the corners of Angie's eyes. "When can we see him?"

Their mother walked out, wiping her eyes. "He wants to see all of you separately. You first, Angie."

"Me first? Why?"

"You're the oldest," Harper said. "Go on."

Angie trudged into the room her mother had exited.

Her strong and robust father—the daddy who'd swung her high in the air and caught his little princess in his arms—lay motionless, helpless.

"Oh, Daddy." She sat in the chair next to him and took his hand.

"My princess," he said, his voice cracked and hoarse. "I want you to know, I didn't—" He coughed.

"Don't, Daddy. It's all right."

"I didn't...change the will. I never would have."

"It's okay. I understand. You wanted what's best for me. I've been a spoiled brat. But I'm learning. I won't let you down."

"I know you won't. You're a good girl, princess. Good and strong. You can handle Bay Crossing. Harper's needed here at Cha Cha, and it will be his one day. Catie will stay at McCray Landing with Chad. So though she'll have an interest in Bay Crossing, it'll be yours." He coughed again.

"You're talking too much," Angie said.

"Yes, I'm afraid you are, Mr. Bay," a nurse said as she entered. "Your monitors are going crazy outside."

"Daddy," Angie said. "I know all this. Don't try to talk anymore. Just let me say a few things."

He nodded, and the nurse left.

"I love you, Daddy. No one could have asked for a better father. You think you spoiled me, but I'm okay now, I promise. I'll handle everything that comes my way." She smiled and squeezed his hand. "And I have a secret. Promise you won't tell anyone."

"I promise," he ground out.

"I'm in love, Daddy. Completely in love for the first time, and it's because of you. Because you made me see what a spoiled little brat I had become. So I started changing my attitude, and I found love."

His cracked lips looked like they were trying to smile.

"Good, princess. Good. You deserve the best."

"I love you so much, Daddy." Tears streamed down her face as she pressed her lips to his cheek. She wanted to stay, wanted to hold him to her forever. But Harper and Catie were waiting. There wasn't much time. She blinked her eyes and steeled her resolve. "Goodbye, Daddy."

"Goodbye, princess," he whispered.

She hurried out of the room so he wouldn't see her break down. He needed her strength. Her father was the strongest man she knew, but what he had to do now took the most courage anyone possessed.

He needed the strength to die.

CHAPTER TEN

Three hours later, it was over.

Angie drove home. In an ivory daze, she showered and put on some sweats. Then she lay on her bed and cried herself to sleep.

She woke up to her cell phone. Didn't bother looking at the number.

"Hello?"

"Angie?"

Rafe.

"I got your number from Amber. Are you standing me up?"

Our dinner date. "I'm sorry, Rafe. I should have called but I fell asleep. My...my father passed away today."

Silence. Then, "Oh God, baby, I'm so sorry. I didn't know he was ill."

"I didn't know either, until yesterday." *But I should have known.* "He kept it from us. That's why I came to you last night. I couldn't be alone. And this morning I wanted to talk."

"I know. I should have let you talk. I should have talked to you last night. I shouldn't have taken advantage of you like that."

She let out a huff and shook her head. "You didn't take advantage of me. I wanted you. I think that was pretty obvious."

"I understand. Making love is the ultimate sign of life. It made sense for you to want it in the face of death."

No, no. He had it all wrong! She hadn't wanted to make love. She'd specifically wanted to make love with *him*. She loved him.

Yet she hadn't told him any of that yet. And right now, she didn't have the energy to confess her love and face that he might not return her feelings. That would take more strength than she possessed at this moment.

"Angie, have you eaten anything today?"

"No."

"I'm coming over and bringing you dinner."

"But—"

"No argument. I made some great stuffed pork chops and homemade applesauce. Good old comfort food. You'll love it. I'll pick up some wine on the way."

"Rafe, I don't know. I'm a mess."

"I don't care. I'll be there in half an hour."

Course he had no idea where she lived. Probably got that information from Amber too.

Amber. She should call Amber. But she couldn't find the strength to even press speed dial. Catie would let their friend know. She wasn't as broken up as Angie was. Catie loved their daddy, Angie knew, but she wasn't as close to him. Besides, she was married now. She had Chad. And their baby on the way.

Who did Angie have?

Harper. Harper was strong. He'd help her get through this. But he was her baby brother.

She needed strong arms to hold her while she cried, a soothing voice to tell her everything would be okay, even when she knew it wouldn't be.

A knock on the door interrupted her thoughts. *Rafe.*

The door squeaked open. "Angie?"

His voice sent ripples through her. Even in her discombobulated state he affected her. "I'm up here."

Sounds came from the kitchen, and then the stairs creaked as Rafe ascended. She looked a fright, but she didn't care. Either he loved her or he didn't. Or he could grow to love her or he couldn't. This was Angelina Bay at her worst. If he couldn't take it, she'd be better off without him. Though she couldn't bear that possibility.

He peeked into her room. "Hey there."

"Hi, Rafe."

"Oh, baby." He came to her, sat down on the bed and took one hand in his. "I am so, so sorry. You must have loved your daddy a lot."

The damn broke. She cried all the tears she'd tried to cry during the afternoon when all she could muster were silent weeps. She cried for her daddy, for herself, for any children she might have who'd never know their wonderful grandpa. She cried for her mama, for her loss, even though they hadn't had a marriage of passion. They'd had a marriage of respect and deep friendship. She cried for Catie and Harper. But mostly she cried for herself and how no one would ever adore her the way Wayne Alan Bay had.

She cried, and she cried, and she cried.

Rafe's black shirt was a mass of tears and nose drippings by the time she finally quieted.

"It's okay." His voice soothed her. "It's going to be okay, baby."

He held her then, held her and rocked her as she choked back the sobs that threatened to unleash again.

Finally, he spoke. "Can you eat something? You should eat."

She shook her head. The thought of food turned her stomach. "Not hungry."

"Okay."

He didn't push her, thank goodness. He'd made her dinner, and she loved him for it. For that and so many other things. For what a good man he was, his amazing work ethic, his devotion to his father, his devotion to the livestock he cared for at Chad's. Mostly she loved him because he was Rafe.

The man she adored.

"Here," he said. He arranged a few pillows and blankets and tucked her under them. Then he lay down next to her and gathered her in his arms.

"Go to sleep."

And she did.

★ ★ ★

She awoke to Rafe still beside her. He'd taken off his jeans and shirt and wore only navy blue boxer briefs. She got up and headed to the bathroom. Looking in the mirror shocked her. What a freaking mess. How could he have stayed?

But then, she loved him. She no longer cared what he looked like. She loved the Rafe inside. If he looked a mess she'd love him just as much. Was it possible he could feel the same for her? Would she ever have the courage to find out?

She jumped in the shower. The water pulsing down her tired body soothed her aches. She closed her eyes and let the warmth coat her hair.

"Like some company?"

She opened her eyes. Rafe, naked and glorious, stood outside her shower, his hand holding the open door.

She motioned him in. He'd taken his hair out of the ponytail, and it hung in glorious tresses down his back.

"Here, let me help," he said. He grabbed shampoo from the shelf and massaged a generous dollop into his hands. He spread it onto her hair and began to massage her scalp.

Judy offered scalp massage for an extra ten dollars at the salon, and Angie took it when she had the time. But Rafe's fingers were in a class all their own. He kneaded her head and neck and pulled the suds though her strands all the way to the ends. She savored the feel of his fingers, the warmth of his presence.

"Now rinse," he said, turning her toward the shower spray. He massaged the suds right out of her hair, squeezed conditioner into his hand, and stroked it into her hair. "Your hair is beautiful, Angie."

"Mmm." She closed her eyes and let his fingers tantalize her. "So's yours. You look like a Lakota warrior, all fierce and wild and free."

"I am part Lakota Sioux."

"Yeah, I know."

"Really? How?"

She jerked her eyes open. Would he think she'd been asking questions about him? "Catie told me."

"Oh." He rinsed the last of the conditioner from her hair. "My other half is Comanche, on my dad's side. My mom is Sioux with a little Irish mixed in." He squeezed some shower gel onto her mesh body scrubber and started washing her. "So where do you come from?"

"Mmm, that feels good. The Bays are English with a little French. My mama was born Maria Ciara Gomez. Her father was Mexican and her mother Irish."

"Maria Ciara, that's pretty."

She closed her eyes, relaxing. "She was named after her two grandmothers, so she named me after my two grandmothers. Angelina was my father's mother, and my middle name is Siobhan, for my mother's mother."

"Beautiful name for a beautiful woman." He rinsed the soap from her body.

Her nipples tightened as the streams of water wandered over her. Why on earth was she getting turned on when she was so sad?

Because this was the man she loved, the man who offered her comfort. If being with him, his body inside her, offered her comfort, why should she not avail herself of it when she so needed it? She reached between his legs and stroked his already erect cock.

"Oh, baby." He gritted his teeth. "Are you sure?"

"Completely."

He lifted her into his arms and impaled her.

Completion again. Sweet, lovely joining.

He grabbed her ass, lifted her up, and thrust her down upon him. Up, down. Up, down, and with each slick stroke, she fell more and more in love with him. So in love she wasn't sure she could continue to live if he weren't here.

"God, you feel good, baby. So good."

She sobbed into his shoulder as her climax built. When it finally emerged and the kaleidoscope of pleasure whirled through her, she murmured into his neck, though not giving voice to her words.

I love you, I love you, I love you.

"Yeah, that's it. Come for me, baby." He hoisted her up and down more rapidly. "God, yeah. I'm coming with you, Angie.

Ah!"

With one final plunge, he pulsed into her. So in tune with him was she, her walls felt every spasm.

He kissed the top of her head as she slid down his slick body.

"Go on and dry off," he said. "If you stay in here with me I might never get to work today."

"But we didn't wash you yet."

"I can handle it myself. If you put your hands on me I may have to fuck you again."

"What would be wrong with that?"

"I can't lose my job." He smiled. "Don't worry, there's plenty of time for more showers."

"Good." She stepped out of the stall and grabbed a towel. "Because I want to get my fingers in that gorgeous hair of yours."

She dried off. He'd said there'd be more showers. That was a good sign. She sighed and got dressed.

She had to admit she felt better. A good night's sleep and a good cry always helped. Not to mention a good bout of lovemaking.

She wasn't looking forward to today. She had to go with her mother to make the cremation and memorial service arrangements.

"You look nice," Rafe said, exiting the bathroom with a towel wrapped around his waist.

His bronze chest glistened. No hair covered it, and only soft hair covered his muscular legs. God, his legs. So powerful as he sauntered toward her. The muscles in his calves bulged. No wonder he could ride a horse without reins.

Speaking of... "I can't make my lesson today. I have to help my mother with the...arrangements."

"Of course. I figured as much."

"But I will continue the lessons. I swear it. It was my father's wish that I learn to ride well, and I intend to."

"Good. I'll enjoy seeing you. But for now, you take a break. You let me know when you want to start lessons again. I'll make sure Belle gets her exercise."

He'd enjoy seeing her at lessons? Did that mean he didn't intend to see her anywhere else? Course he'd just said there'd be more showers. *Quit second guessing, Angie.*

"Can I get you something for breakfast before you go to work?" she asked.

He shook his head. "I will take some of my leftover dinner for lunch though."

His dinner. "I'm so sorry. You went to all that trouble to make me dinner and I—"

He stopped her with a chaste kiss on the mouth. "Don't you worry about that. You had much bigger things on your mind last night, and you can enjoy the other half of the leftovers for your own lunch."

"Can I get a rain check?" Did she sound too desperate?

"Sure. Of course. As soon as you're feeling up to it. But don't rush it, Angie. Take your time to grieve."

"Well"—her voice shook—"I still need to eat."

"True enough. Make sure you do. You'll be able to deal with things a lot better if you don't starve yourself."

He hadn't taken the hint. Oh, well. Maybe he was right. She needed to take time for herself and her family so they could all get through the next couple of weeks. She'd miss him, but her family needed her and she needed them.

Daddy, I miss you so.

CHAPTER ELEVEN

Who was that man? A nice-looking older man, black hair going white at the temples, loitered around the buffet table in the dining room. Angie didn't recall seeing him at the memorial service. Course she hadn't been overly aware of her surroundings. Saying goodbye to her father had taken all her strength. Part of her still couldn't quite grasp that he was gone.

The man looked somewhat familiar, but she couldn't say how.

Her mother swayed next to her. "Good Lord."

"Who is it, Mama?"

"I'm not quite sure. But I think it's your uncle."

"I have an uncle?"

"Yes. Your father's brother."

"I never knew Daddy had a brother."

"He never spoke of him. He forbade mention of his name. They had a huge falling out when they were young. Jeff got into big trouble with the law and went to prison. Your great-grandfather disinherited him."

"Why is he here now?"

"I don't have any idea. I sincerely don't." She leaned onto Angie. "I need to sit down."

"Of course." She turned to Harper. "Take Mama out of here. She's had enough. I need to see what this man wants."

"I'll come with you. Wait just a minute." Harper ushered Maria out of the living room and up the stairs. Five minutes later, he returned.

"Okay," he said. "Let's see what this guy wants."

They approached the strange man who was helping himself to some honey ham from the buffet table.

"Good afternoon, I'm Harper Bay." Harper held out his hand.

"Jefferson Bay," the man said, "and this must be the lovely Angelina?"

Angie nodded. "What are you doing here?"

"Why, I've come to pay my respects to my brother and his family, of course. I'm your uncle."

"So our mother informed us," Harper said. "Any reason you can think of why our father neglected to mention you all these years?"

"It's a long story. I need to sit down with you two and your mother. Where's the other sister?"

"She's over there." Harper pointed to Catie. "That's her husband, Chad McCray."

"Yeah, I heard she married pretty young. Too bad for me. But you're still single, right?" he asked Angie.

Why on earth would he care if Catie was married? "I'm not sure what business it could possibly be of yours, but yes, I'm single."

Rafe approached them, Amber and Tom on his heels. "You okay, Angie?" he asked. "You look a little pale."

"I just buried my daddy."

"I know. Just...you look like you could use some sittin' time." He took her arm. "Excuse us please."

"Wait a minute. I'd like to meet your friends, Angelina," Jefferson said.

Rafe stuck out his hand. "I'm Rafe Grayhawk. This is

my brother, Tom, and this is Amber Cross. We're friends of Angie's."

"A pleasure. I'm Angelina's uncle, Jefferson Bay."

"Nice to meet you. But Angie really needs to sit down. Come on, honey."

Rafe led her to a sofa in the hallway where, thank the lord, no one was loitering.

"I don't want to insult your family on such a sad day but your uncle could use some manners. He didn't seem concerned about your well-being at all."

"Why should he? He just met me today."

"What?"

"Seriously. Till today, I never knew he existed. My daddy never mentioned a brother. I thought he was an only child."

Rafe's eyebrows rose. "Interesting time for him to show up."

"I know. He says he needs to talk to us. I have no idea what it could be about."

"Probably just wants to make amends."

"Hopefully. But wouldn't it have made more sense for him to come around while Daddy was alive?" She massaged her temples and closed her eyes.

Rafe's fingers softly drifted over her forearm. "You want to go upstairs and lie down? Get on out of here for a little while?"

His touch was soothing. Felt so nice.

"You have no idea how much I want to do that, but I can't. Mama's already gone upstairs, so I have to play hostess."

"A lady who just lost her father doesn't have to stand on ceremony, baby. Let's get you upstairs."

She relented. What the heck? Harper and Catie could take care of things. And mama's sister, Aunt Meghan, was here to assist. Catie's two sisters-in-law, Dusty and Annie, were helping too. She took Rafe's arm and let him lead her upstairs.

"Which room?"

"First one the right," she said. "That was my room as a kid."

She grimaced as her pink canopy bed came into view. But she was too sad and tired to care what Rafe might think of her childhood tastes, though she did wonder for a moment why Maria had never changed any of their rooms. Catie's still had stuffed horses strewn all over.

Rafe seemed undaunted, though, and helped her lie down amid the fluff. "You stay here for a while. If you're needed downstairs, I'll come get you." He gave her a chaste kiss on the forehead, shut the blinds on the windows, and left quietly.

Angie slept until morning.

★ ★ ★

She woke to her blinds opened. "Wake up, sleepyhead," Harper said, shoving her blinds up. "Our esteemed uncle's coming in an hour to talk to us about God knows what."

"Harp, geez! I have to go home and shower and change."

"Hurry it up then. Be back here by two o'clock."

"Two o'clock? It can't possibly be one."

"It is, Sis. You've been up here twenty hours or so, give or take a minute or two."

"Can't this wait? We just buried our father, for God's sake."

"Believe me, I told him that. He says he has to talk to us now. That it's urgent."

"Is Catie coming over?"

"She and Chad are already here, downstairs."

Angie looked down at her wrinkled black suit. "I can't wear this. Tell you what, go get something out of Mama's closet for me, will you? Nothing too frumpy."

"Since when does our mother dress like a frump? I'll have Catie pick something. You get in the shower and get cleaned up."

Thank goodness her bathroom was still fully stocked. The shower warmed and massaged her aching body.

She dressed in a beige pantsuit that Catie must have set on her bed while she was showering and then walked downstairs. She found her mother, brother, sister, Chad, and Uncle Jefferson in the room that had been her father's office. Jefferson sat behind her father's desk.

A shiver niggled at the back of her neck. This felt all wrong.

"Ah, the lovely Angelina," Uncle Jefferson said, "my mother's namesake."

"Yes. Uh...hello."

"Sit down. You of all people will be the most interested in what I have to say."

Angie gulped. What on earth did he mean?

"Have a seat, my dear." Jefferson pointed to an empty chair.

Angie sat, still in a daze from the memorial. "What's this all about?"

"We have no idea," Harper said. "He wouldn't tell us till we were all here." He turned to his uncle. "We're all here now. Let's get on with it."

"Of course." Jefferson set a document on the desk. "You might be wondering what this is."

"Not really," Harper said.

"You will in a minute. Before I read it to you, I want to tell you all a little story."

"How about you tell us why none of us knew you existed till now?" Harper said, his voice not happy.

"You knew I existed, didn't you, Mia?"

Mia? Angie had never heard anyone but her father refer to her mother as Mia.

Maria Bay rose. "We've all been through the wringer, Jeff. Please just tell us why you're here."

"Simmer down and I'll get to that."

Maria sat back down and sighed. Angie regarded her mother's pale cheeks. None of them needed this stress, especially Maria.

"Now, for my tale of two brothers. Once there were two brothers, the good son and the bad son. I think you know who the good son was. The esteemed Wayne Alan Bay. As you know, Wayne and I were orphaned when he was ten and I was eight. We were raised by our grandfather, Norman Bay, on the western slope ranch that your father now owns, Bay Crossing. This"—he held up the document again—"is the last will and testament of Norman Bay."

"So what?" Harper said.

"You'll see its importance momentarily," Jeff said. "Grandpa ruled us with an iron hand, and Wayne, the good son, was held in high favor. Jeff, the bad son, was a rebel. He shirked his duties around the ranch, got in trouble with the law on more than one occasion, but finally found the will to turn his life around when he met the woman of his dreams."

A choking sob came from her mother's throat. Angie looked over, and Maria had buried her face in her hands.

"Mama? What is it?" she asked.

Maria shook her head.

"Our mother's been through hell," Harper said. "Now what is this all about?"

"Alas," Jeff continued, "the woman betrayed him in the worst possible way."

Maria lifted her head. "Please, Jeff. Don't do this."

"His sweet angel betrayed him by sleeping with his own brother!"

Angie gasped. She looked at her brother and her sister and Chad. All looked equally shocked.

"Mama?" Catie's soft voice echoed through the room.

"Why? Why now, Jeff? We thought you were long gone. No one has heard from you in decades. We assumed you'd died in prison."

"Prison?" Harper's voice was shaky.

"Yes, prison," Jeff said. "I was sentenced to life in prison for a crime I did not commit."

"Then why did you plead guilty?" Maria shook her head. "You mean you didn't murder that man?"

Jeff shook his head. "Of course I didn't. I'm not a killer. I pleaded guilty because I had nothing left to live for. The evidence against me was overwhelming, and my own grandfather had already disinherited me. He had already tried and convicted me. When I found out you had slept with Wayne and were carrying his child, I had nothing left at all."

"Then what happened? How did you get out?"

"Three years ago, a man approached me in prison. Said he could no longer live with the lies. He told the truth, and DNA evidence further proved my innocence."

"Hold on, hold on," Harper said. "There's a whole lot to this story you're not telling us."

"Go to the library and look it up," Jeff said. "It's a chapter in my life I'd rather forget, and it has little to do with why I'm here."

"Then let's get to that, please." Harper stood. "Why are you here?"

"Sit your ass down, young man. This has little to do with you. We are here because of this document." He rustled the papers. "Grandpa Norman's will."

"Your grandfather's been dead for over twenty years," Maria said. "You said yourself he disinherited you. Bay Crossing went to Wayne, and now it belongs to Angelina and Caitlyn. You can look at Wayne's will."

"Only the girls? What about your handsome son, there?" He motioned to Harper who was still standing, gripping the back of his chair, his knuckles white.

"Not that it's any of your business," Maria said, "but I inherited this ranch from a childless relative. I transferred it to Wayne, and he made the decision to bequeath it to Harper and Bay Crossing to the girls. He felt a man should have his own ranch, and this ranch is roughly equal to half of what the other is worth, so it all came out fairly."

"Ah, yes, dear old Wayne, always fair."

"I'm sure I sound like an echo in here," Harper said, "but your point?"

"My point, dear nephew, is that my grandfather was not only an arrogant bastard, he was also one of the premier male chauvinist pigs of our time." He laughed. "I confess I never thought his old school sexism would work in my favor, but I'm happy to tell you I was wrong." He stood and handed the will to Harper. "I hear you're an attorney."

Harper took the paper. "Yes, I am."

"Then I refer you to section thirteen B of the document."

Harper rustled the papers, his eyes scanning the document. His eyebrows shot up. "Oh, shit."

"What is it, Harper?" Maria asked.

"It seems there's a section here that may supersede Dad's intentions. Norman Bay did grant Bay Crossing to Dad, but left a limitation on his ownership and ability to bequeath it to his own heirs."

"I'm not sure I follow," Maria said.

"Jefferson is right. Norman was a chauvinist." Harper cleared his throat. "Dad can only bequeath the property on the western slope to sons or married daughters. Any daughter who is not yet married can't inherit, and that portion reverts to any other living issue of Norman's body, by representation, which is, in this case, Jefferson."

Angie's stomach plummeted.

She was the problem. The unmarried daughter. Harper got Cha Cha. Catie got half of Bay Crossing.

Angie got nothing.

CHAPTER TWELVE

Nothing.

She had no marketable skills, no job, no income, no husband.

She had nothing.

Angie sat frozen to her chair. She opened her mouth to speak, but no words emerged. The irony of her situation gripped her like a fever. Her father had insisted she learn to ride, learn to ranch, or he'd disinherit her. He'd died before he could make good on his threat, and then said he wouldn't have done it.

She'd been disinherited anyway.

"Harper," Maria said, "there must be something we can do."

Jefferson smiled sardonically. "This doesn't affect you, pretty girl," he said to Catie, "since you had the good sense to marry that cowboy of yours. Your sister, on the other hand, is shit outta luck."

"Do not address my wife again," Chad McCray said. "You won't get away with this. The McCrays own half of this town."

"Simmer down, McCray," Jefferson said. "This doesn't concern you or your wife. As for what you own, your wife, not you, owns half of Bay Crossing. The other half belongs to me."

Catie clenched her fists and stood. "We won't let you do this to Angie." She clutched her belly.

"You all right?" Chad rose and helped her back to her

chair.

"I'm fine. Just a little light-headed."

"Come on," Chad said. "We're leaving." He turned to Maria. "My brothers and I will help in any way we can, I promise you that. But right now I want Catie away from this stress."

Maria nodded. "I understand completely. Go."

Catie balked, but eventually relented. "Call me as soon as he leaves."

"I will." Marie shut the door behind them. "Now"—her brown eyes flared—"let's get to the bottom of this once and for all, Jeff. You will not punish me by doing this to my daughter." Her fists clenched. Sweat beaded on her brow. "You won't, I tell you."

Jefferson's eyes didn't waver. They were hard eyes. Eyes that had been to prison. Eyes that had seen things Angie couldn't fathom. For a millisecond, a fraction of sorrow for him tugged at her—until she remembered why he was here.

To steal everything she had. Or never had.

He spoke, his voice terse. "Nothing you can do about it, Mia. Sorry."

Harper glanced through the rest of the document, his brown eyes misting. *He feels bad for me. He wants to help me.*

"Ah-ha!"

"What, did you find something?" Maria's voice shook with a dash of hope.

"There's reference to a codicil here," Harper said, nodding to Jeff. "Did you bother to read that?"

"What codicil? I didn't find any codicil."

"We need to search this office," Harper said. "Dad kept all his important papers in these files." He walked to an oak filing cabinet and starting opening drawers and shuffling through documents.

He pulled out a file folder. "Here's the will. I guess Dad never bothered to read it." He pushed it aside and pulled out another document. "And here's the codicil, dated the same date as the will and signed and notarized." He scanned the document. His lips curved upward in a caustic grin and he waved the document in Jefferson's face. "Don't get too comfortable with the idea of property ownership, Uncle Jeff. Angie has two months from the date of Dad's death to marry. If she does, she still inherits."

"What?" Jefferson grabbed the codicil. "That can't be."

"Read it yourself."

"Damn it! I want a lawyer to look at this."

"I *am* a lawyer. You can take it to Denver and have some expensive downtown attorney look at it and tell you the same thing if you want. But I have the same education they do."

"You're a ranch lawyer."

"I'm a rancher with a legal education and a license to practice law in this state, the state where that document was written, signed, and notarized. It doesn't take a classy downtown office to read a will and codicil. It takes one year of law school. I have three."

"Well, then," Maria said, her body limp, "we'll just have to find Angie a husband. Shouldn't be too difficult. She's a beautiful girl."

Angie sat, numb. "Sure, just put me up on the auction block. Marry Angelina Bay and inherit half a ranch."

How had her life come to this?

"Angie, there are a hundred men in town who'd love to marry you," her mother said, her voice now louder, a little calmer.

But she didn't want a hundred men. She wanted just one man. And damn it, she didn't want a marriage like her parents'. She wanted love.

Ice settled in her arms, and her head swam with visions of wills and codicils and horrible long lost uncles. What would she do?

★ ★ ★

Angie wasn't exactly sure how she got home to change into riding clothes, how she got to Belle's stall. As she groomed the sleek ebony coat, her mind wandered to the days when she was a little girl, the days spent with her doting daddy. Riding in front of him in the saddle across the expanse of their property on the western slope. The sweet aroma of the peach trees in bloom in the springtime, and the rocky terrain of the vineyards in summer. And the cattle of course, not as sweet smelling, but the pride of Daddy's ranch. Best beef on the western slope, rivaled in Colorado only by the McCrays here on this side of the Rockies.

When Mama had inherited the ranch here, they named it Cha Cha, for Caitlyn, Harper, and Angelina. A ridiculous name, Angie always thought, but indicative of how much she and her siblings meant to their parents. They'd decided to move here so they'd be closer to the big city of Denver where she and Harper could have better schooling. Catie hadn't yet been a year old, and she didn't remember ever living on the western slope.

But Angie did. She'd loved it there. Loved the fresh peaches and apples every fall, the acres upon acres of fresh green orchards. She'd had a pony named Lucas who Daddy had helped her learn to ride. Course Belle was far more beautiful and valuable than Lucas. Why had she stopped riding?

Why had she stopped doing a lot of things?

The urge to ride with the wind hit her like the gush of a storm. Catie always rode when she needed to escape. She said riding was better than shopping any day.

Oh Lord, do I need an escape right now.

She saddled Belle and led her out of the stable. So she didn't have her helmet. No matter. Riding would come back to her. And she'd had a few lessons. She could click her tongue and get Belle to walk. No problem.

She mounted the mare and practiced the leg exercises Rafe had taught her. Belle circled to the left, and then to the right.

"Good girl," Angie said.

But circles weren't helping her escape. She wanted to ride. Preferably over the horizon to a place free from heartache and worry.

She clicked to Belle and let the mare walk away from the practice area. What a gentle horse. She let Belle move into a trot. That was it. She couldn't handle anything more. No cantering or galloping. The trot was nice, though her butt was bouncing up and down on the saddle. Not good. She gripped her legs around Belle's girth and tried to steady herself.

So far so good.

The McCray ranch was beautiful. Green and plentiful, cattle and horses grazing. Fresh late summer air. The golden warmth of the late afternoon sun heated her cheeks. Yes, she could enjoy this. Why, she asked herself again, had she ever stopped riding?

Daddy'd been right. She should have learned about ranch life long before now. Course what good would it have done her? She no longer owned a ranch. Not unless she could find someone to marry her in the next few months. How in the hell would she do that?

She'd have to marry not for love, but for convenience, like her parents had.

She thought for a moment. Daddy's brother had been in love with Mama. Could Mama have been in love with him too?

She shook her head. Mama had slept with Daddy, and she, Angie, was the result. Perhaps Mama had never known of Jefferson's feelings. Yet she hadn't seemed surprised when he'd brought up the story in the office.

What else didn't she know about her mother and father? She wasn't sure she wanted to know anything more. She'd rather remember her daddy as the kind and loving man he'd been.

She rode and she rode. The orange sun sank lower in the sky. Time to turn back. How long had she been riding? She had no idea. She hadn't worn a watch, and she'd left her cell phone in Belle's stall. She hadn't wanted to be bothered with anything this afternoon.

Hadn't wanted to think about her future. Or lack thereof.

Hadn't wanted to think about the possibility of an arranged marriage, when she only wanted marriage to one man.

She gasped in a breath.

Why not?

She could propose to Rafe. She could explain her situation. Maybe he'd marry her. Even if he didn't love her yet, he could grow to love her. And she could help him. Her ranch could help him. Her money could help buy that place in Arizona he wanted for his father. He'd own his own ranch—well, half. But Catie and Chad would be here, so it would, for all intent and purpose, be their ranch. Hers and Rafe's.

Excited at the thought, she urged Belle into a gallop before she realized her mistake.

Oh no! Belle was going so fast, and Angie's bottom was already sore from the trotting.

Maintain, Angie, maintain. It's not like you've never been on a horse before. You can control her.

She pulled back on the reins. Rafe would hate her for this. He hated reins. Thank God she'd used a bit today.

Belle whinnied and didn't slow.

Come on, girl. Slow down!

Angie tried the reins again.

Again.

No effect.

Belle was running free as the wind and clearly had no intention of stopping. The poor thing was probably tired of trotting for so long.

Angie didn't think she was in any immediate danger. Why not enjoy it? She'd deal with her sore ass later.

Strands of hair came loose from her twin ponytails and whipped her in the face. Freeing. Exhilarating. The wind rushed at her. Specks of who knows what sanded her face. Instant exfoliation! The nature surrounding her ran past her as if in motion itself, tantalized her, made her forget her troubles. Finally, when Belle seemed to be relaxing, she tried the reins again.

Success.

Belle slowed to a canter and then back to a trot.

"Good girl," she said, petting Belle's mane, which was now knotted and tangled from the ride. "That's my good girl."

"Angie, what the hell are you doing?"

Rafe's voice. He galloped up on Adonis and stopped beside her. He wore no hat. His onyx hair had come loose and blew around his face. His forearms were clenched and sinewy. Lord, he was beautiful.

"Thank God. I've been worried sick."

"Worried?"

"No one knows where you are. Catie and Chad are frantic, and when I saw Belle was gone—"

"I'm fine. You taught me well."

His facial muscles tightened, and his lips formed a taut line. "Damn it, I taught you how to ride in circles. You were nowhere near ready to ride alone. That horse could have thrown you. It could have... God I can't even think about it."

"She's a gentle horse. She wouldn't throw me."

"Look at you. You're a mess. The horse is a mess. You've been running wild."

"Yes, and it felt amazing." She wasn't about to apologize. Belle was her horse, after all. "Just what I needed today."

He brushed his hair out of his eyes. "Angie, I know you're upset about your dad. I understand. I really do. But that doesn't mean you should go out and kill yourself. Christ."

She sighed and shook her head, letting her loose hair whip her cheeks. "It felt wonderful, Rafe. I can't wait to ride more. I honestly don't know why I ever stopped."

"Fine. You can ride whenever you want. As long as I, or someone equally qualified, is with you. Never alone again. Not till I tell you you're ready."

"Please, you don't own me."

He ignored her taunt. "Follow me. Stick to a trot. I'll lead you back to the stable."

An hour later Belle was safely bedded, and Angie faced a still very angry Rafe.

"I ought to put you over my knee and give you a thrashing," he said.

She smiled and arched one brow. "Whatever you're into."

"Damn it!" He pounded his fist into the wall of the stable. "I was worried sick. I didn't know what to do."

"I'm fine. There was never anything to worry—"

He slammed his mouth onto hers and forced her lips open. This was no gentle kiss. It was meant to chasten. An angry, punishing kiss. He thrust his tongue into her mouth, drinking of her as though he were dying of thirst.

She melted into his anger, into his possession, into his punishment. The kiss drugged her with angry passion, fierce possession.

It was the kiss of a man who'd feared for her safety, who now reveled in her return.

The kiss of a man in love?

Could he love her?

Her life would be complete if he did. He'd marry her. Save her ranch. She'd have a real marriage, too, not a marriage like her parents'.

His assault on her mouth continued. With one hand, he gripped her breast like a vise. It hurt, but oh God, it hurt so good.

His fingers found her nipple through the fabric of her blouse and bra and pinched. Sweet burn, sweet pain, sweet ecstasy.

His other hand forced her legs open and plunged inside

her jeans. He found her clit and fingered it roughly, groaning into her mouth.

He ripped his mouth from hers, his black eyes blazing.

"You're coming home with me."

CHAPTER THIRTEEN

Angie woke in the middle of an amazing orgasm. Rafe's tongue darted between her legs, driving her to a frenzy.

Last night he'd stripped her naked and thrust into her wet heat without any foreplay. It had been mad, passionate love, and she'd soared to the stars despite the violent nature—in fact, had fallen all the more in love at his possession of her.

"I'm sorry I was so rough," he'd said after his completion, holding her gently in his strong muscular arms.

"Don't be," she'd said. "It was incredible."

He'd smiled at her then, a smile that made her heart race and stop at the same time.

"You're amazing."

She'd chuckled and kissed his nose. "Sometime I might just take you up on that thrashing you promised."

His laugh had reverberated through the room. "You will, huh?"

"Yes, I just might." And she'd meant it. A little spanking sounded like a real turn on to this spoiled little brat.

Rafe continued to pleasure her, his fingers stretching her channel, finding that special spot that made her go mad with pleasure.

"You taste so good, baby," he said against her folds, his voice a soft vibration, his breath a dulcet caress. "Mmm, I love it when you squirt."

So did she. It was like an orgasm but different—not quite

a climax, but a rush of endorphins, as though her whole body levitated and took flight. Something she'd only experienced with Rafe. The man she loved.

"You're beautiful down here. Perfectly pink and plump."

Ah! His fingers again. Her whole body tensed and then melted into oblivion. Over and over again. *Too much. Must stop. No. Never, never stop.*

"You're so hot, baby," he said. "So fucking hot."

Still his fingers probed, his tongue lapped. Still she came, again and again. When he finally paused for a breath, she was spent.

"Come here, Rafe. Please. I need you inside me."

"Oh, baby," he groaned.

He slid up her body and thrust into her.

So sensitive was her sex, so swollen, his intrusion was almost painful. But in a good way. Such a good way. A way she wanted to feel for the rest of her life, and then some.

He thrust and thrust and finally groaned on top of her and convulsed.

So wonderful. If only he were hers...

He rolled off her a few minutes later.

"Hungry?"

Not really. She hadn't eaten much since she'd found out about her father. "No," she said, and her tummy let out a growl.

"Oh, you're not, huh?" He laughed. "Sit tight. I'll be back in a few minutes with some breakfast."

It was his day off, so he didn't have to leave her at the crack of dawn as usual. He brought back scrambled eggs and toast.

"I figured you might be embarrassed to come out to the kitchen with Tom being here and all."

She laughed. "I'm fine. No worries. Though this is good,

because I'd rather be alone with you."

"You read my mind." He kissed her lips and then fed her a spoonful of eggs. "Good?"

She swallowed and licked her lips. Tasted like sawdust. "You're a great cook."

"How did you like my chops?"

Angie stiffened and waved away the next bite of eggs. "I'm sorry. I didn't try them. I just haven't felt much like eating since the whole thing with Daddy."

"It's okay. I understand. Next time I cook for you though, I expect you to eat hearty."

"I guess this is the next time then."

"Hell, eggs don't count. I'll have you know I'm a pretty fair cook."

"Me too," she joked. "I make great JELL-O."

"Well, you'll learn."

Learn to cook? Why should he care? Unless... She needed to talk to him. Explain her little problem.

Her cell phone buzzed. She fumbled on the nightstand where she'd left it.

Harper.

"Excuse me for a sec," she said to Rafe as he set a plate of eggs in front of her. "Hey, Harp. What's up?"

"Good news. We got you a date."

"Date for what?"

"For meeting a husband, silly. You don't think we're going to let our ranch go to that idiot uncle who emerged from a crack in hell, do you?"

Her throat constricted. "Uh, I'm not sure what you mean."

"Tonight Frank Longhorn's coming over."

Frank Longhorn? Seriously? He had his own damn ranch.

What did he need with hers? And his ears stuck out.

"He's been mooning over you for years," Harper continued.

"Not interested."

He laughed. "We figured you'd say that. That's why Joe Bradley and Beau Stevens are also coming."

"The mechanic and the chef?"

"Yep. Just think—you'll either get free car fixing for life or free gourmet food for life."

"Harper, I'm not interested."

"Look, Angie, no one says you have to stay married. We just need to comply with the will till Uncle Asshole is out of the way."

"I'll find my own husband, thank you very much."

Rafe's eyes turned into dinner plates. *Shit!* What a big mouth she had.

"I've got to go, Harp. I'll talk to you later."

"Be at Ma's at seven sharp."

"God. Whatever. I've got to go."

She clicked the phone off and turned to Rafe. "That's not what it sounded like."

"Yeah?" He fumbled with his fork. "It sounded like you're looking for a husband."

"No, I'm not. That is, I'd rather not be."

"Sorry. I'm not following."

"Oh, Rafe, it's a huge mess." She pushed her plate of eggs away. "And it's a long sordid story."

"I don't have anywhere to be. Do you?"

Just right here. Forever. "No."

"Then tell me if you want to. I'll try to help."

Thing was, he *could* help her. But would he? Slowly, with

some tears she tried to hide unsuccessfully, she poured out the story of Uncle Jefferson Bay and Great-Grandpa's will.

"So if I don't get married in the next two months, I can't inherit my share of the western slope ranch." She sighed. "Simple as that."

Rafe's dark eyes glazed over. What was he thinking? She had no idea, but he didn't look happy.

"I wish there was something I could do to help."

"Well"—she cleared her throat—"there is, actually."

He lowered his gaze. Why wouldn't he look at her?

"I guess it's clear from this story that I need to get married if I want my inheritance. I'm sorry if you think it's part of me being a spoiled brat, but I do want my inheritance. I have no other income." Crap, this didn't make her sound too good. "Don't get me wrong. I have an education in health sciences. I could probably get a job somewhere. I'm not completely useless."

You're babbling, Angie.

He still wasn't looking at her.

"Anyway, my daddy was insistent that I learn to ride well, as you know. And he also wanted me to learn about ranching to prepare me for the inheritance. Of course he didn't know about this thing in his grandpa's will. Otherwise I'm sure he'd have made sure I was married by now. I don't know how, but Daddy would have taken care of everything."

Still babbling.

"Anyway, I guess I need a husband, and I was thinking, you seem to like me a little." She gave what she hoped was a teasing smile.

Still no response. She took a deep breath. Might as well finish up.

"So would you consider it? Marrying me, that is?"

He still studied the sheets.

"Would you at least look at me?"

He looked up, and sadness laced his beautiful dark eyes.

"I'm sorry, Angie, but I can't marry you."

Her heart sank. He didn't love her. The pain wasn't a sharp lance like she thought it would be. It was more like a dull ache, like she'd been punched in the stomach. Still, maybe he didn't understand. After all, she hadn't yet confessed her love to him.

"You don't have to love me, Rafe." *Though I wish you did.* "I just need a husband within two months. This thing with my great-granddaddy's will...it's—" She sighed. "It doesn't say I need to find a husband who loves me. We don't have to stay married. I mean, we should for a while, I guess. For show." *And to give you enough time to fall head over heels in love with me.* "I could help you. The ranch has money. I could help you get that place for your father in Arizona. He could leave here and be healthy again. And—"

He gently placed his fingers over her lips, silencing her.

"I understand, and I wish I could help. But I can't marry you, baby."

"I told you that you don't have to love me. It's a business arrangement."

He shook his head. "Whether I love you isn't the issue." He looked down at the sheets again and then returned his gaze to her.

Were those tears misting in the corner of his eyes?

"Why then? Why can't you marry me?"

His black eyes pierced her own. "Because I'm already married."

CHAPTER FOURTEEN

Could her life get any more screwed up?

Angie rushed to downtown Bakersville and headed to Deb's Boutique. She'd hurriedly put her riding clothes back on, run a brush through her snarled hair, and left, barreling through Rafe's hold as he tried to stop her. Nope, she didn't listen. Didn't want to hear about his so-called wife. So she escaped his grasp and ran. She had no car, no way to get home. Her car was still at Chad and Catie's where she'd left it to go riding yesterday afternoon.

Thankfully, Rafe lived right in town and she could make it to Deb's. She needed shopping. If she'd had her car, she'd have headed straight for Denver where the big department stores were. Yep, she needed *that* kind of shopping. But she'd have to settle for Deb's.

"Angie." Deb eyed her up and down. "Uh...how are you?"

"Is that little redheaded bitch working today?"

"Lori's off today, and I'll thank you—"

"Oh, Deb, spare me the hurt bunny look when I insult your employee. I need a shopping spree."

"Angie, I was so sorry to hear about your father."

"Spare me the feigning sympathy look too, please."

Deb threw her hands up. "Fine. You're the customer. Though why you're wandering around town in wrinkled riding clothes is beyond me. You never allow yourself to look less than perfect."

"There's a first time for everything. What do you have new?"

"Some gorgeous evening wear just came in."

She hadn't been to a good party in months. But why not stock up for her next invite? "Show me something in black. And red. And silver. Short please. I want to show my legs."

"Be right back."

Deb whooshed away while Angie situated herself in the dressing room. More party dresses. Just what she needed.

What was wrong with her? Not only was the man she loved married to someone else, here she was shopping...when she was broke. She wouldn't get her inheritance. How did she expect to pay for these new clothes?

She launched the problem from her mind. She'd worry about that later.

"Here's the first batch," Deb said.

Angie opened the door to the dressing room and grabbed the dresses.

The black one fit like a glove. She'd take it.

The red one was a little too ruffly, but it had a certain girlish look that appealed to her.

She'd take it.

The silver one wasn't quite short enough, but would be gorgeous with strappy sandals in the same color.

She'd take it.

"I'll take these three," she said when Deb come with another armful.

"You'll be happy to know that your friend Lori picked all of those from the last catalogue. I told you she knew about fashion."

Right. The twit knew nothing. The red number was way

too frilly. So why was she buying it again?

Didn't matter. Her daddy always saw that she got what she wanted. But Daddy no longer existed. No one was here to see that she got her ranch.

No one was here to see that she got the man she wanted.

The next dress was all wrong for her.

She'd take it.

"I'm tired of dresses, Deb. I'm coming out. I want shoes to go with these four."

She tried and discarded the first five pairs Deb showed her and then changed her mind. "I'll take these, but now find me something that really screams feet."

Was that an eye roll? Not the way to treat a customer.

Deb came back with a pair of strappy black numbers. "I'm sure you'll find that these are real screamers."

Angie tried them on. The stiletto heel was too high and horribly uncomfortable.

"I'll take them. I want to look at fashion boots next."

She chose a pair of black thigh highs in leather with another stiletto and a pair of sleek silver snakeskin ankle boots.

"Anything else?" Deb asked.

"Yes. Scarves. One to go with each dress I chose. You pick them out."

"Very well." Deb sighed.

Angie put her riding boots back on and wondered how in hell she'd get home. "Put all of this on my bill," she said.

She stood and stared out the window. As luck would have it, Chad and Catie walked out of Rena's Coffee Shop at that instant.

"Hey!" She walked out the door of the boutique. "Catie!"

Catie turned. "Oh, hi, Ang. How are you doing?"

That question was unanswerable at the moment. "Could you guys give me a lift?"

"What?"

They walked toward her. "What's going on?" Chad asked.

"I'm stuck here. My car's out at your place. I took Belle on a ride yesterday afternoon after our meeting with Jeff, and—"

"You left your car at our place?"

"Yeah, it's a long story."

Catie sighed and turned to Chad. "She's had it rough. Let's get her home."

"Sure enough, sugar," Chad said. "Come on, Angie, our car's out back of Rena's."

"I'll be right there. Just let me get the stuff I bought."

Her packages in tow, she ambled behind the storefronts and found Chad and Catie.

"What on earth did you buy?" Catie asked.

"Just some dresses and shoes. And scarves."

"To go with the closet full of dresses and shoes you already own, I presume?" Chad said.

Catie punched him in the arm. "Leave her alone. She was the closest to Daddy, and now this idiot uncle of ours shows up and threatens everything she has."

"Sorry, sugar. Just tryin' to lighten things up a little."

No one spoke the rest of the drive. Angie transferred her purchases to her own car and drove home. She shed the dirty riding clothes and threw them in the trash.

She headed for the shower.

Pelting water soothed her body, but did nothing for her heart and soul. She forced her mind to go numb. She'd think about it tomorrow.

Tomorrow was another day.

She shook her head. Yeah, right. At least Scarlett O'Hara's man hadn't been married to someone else.

Who was she? Why didn't they live together? Were they separated? What was the deal? And why in God's name had he not told her he was married?

Love was crap. She'd marry one of the morons her mother had invited to dinner tonight. Didn't matter.

She got out, dried off, and put on a short silk robe. She went out to the living room to grab her bags when a knock on the door startled her.

Standing behind her door was none other than Rafe Grayhawk.

Her heart lurched, and her nipples tightened against the soft fabric. Even now, he affected her. She should ignore him, but she couldn't.

She opened the door but did not invite him in. "What is it?"

"Hey, baby."

"Don't call me that."

"I want to explain."

"Explain what? That you've been fucking me while you're married to someone else? I already got that, thanks."

"It's not like that."

"Seems to me that's exactly how it is."

"I mean there are circumstances. If I could just come in—"

"No."

"Please."

"I said no." She started to shut the door, but he lodged his foot in it.

"I'm going to talk to you, Angie." He edged her out of the way, entered the room, and looked around. "Been shopping?"

"None of your business."

He shook his head. "Thought you'd been disinherited."

"That's a minor setback. I'll take care of it. My mother's lining up husband candidates for me as we speak."

"Husband candidates?"

"Did I not make myself clear earlier? I need to get married or I lose everything."

He pursed his lips. "You mean you're going to marry someone else?"

"Of course I'm going to marry someone else. I've got to."

"What about us?"

Was he serious? "What about us? You're married. There is no us. There never was."

"I want to explain about that."

"Not interested."

"Damn it." He grabbed her arm. "If you'd stuck around this morning we could have cleared this all up."

"Let go of me," she said through clenched teeth.

He let her go, and she began pulling clothes and shoes out of the bags. "If you'll excuse me, I have to decide on an outfit for tonight. Got to look my best, you know." She held up the strappy stilettos. "These ought to get a few of them interested, don't you think?"

Rafe shook his head. "Baby—"

"I'm not your baby, hand. You're not good enough for me anyway. You never were. You were nothing but a dalliance. Now get on out of here. Go home to your own wife."

Rafe's dark eyes clouded. Well, served him right. He turned and left her home.

She'd told him where to get off. Nothing less than he deserved for keeping such an important fact from her. She'd done the right thing.

So why did she feel like she'd been hit by a truck?

★ ★ ★

Frank Longhorn was as boring as he'd been in high school when he'd nursed a major crush on Angie. And his ears still stuck out like Dumbo's. He was short too. She towered over him in her stilettos.

Joe Bradley did clean up well. His dark blond hair was pulled back in a low ponytail—the same way Rafe wore his. Yes, he was attractive, but he was no Rafe.

None of them were.

She cornered her mother in the kitchen. "I can't do this, Mama."

"Angie, you have no choice."

"Yes, I do. I'll be disinherited, I guess. I can still live here with you, right?"

"Of course you can. As long as I have a home, you will always have one."

"Thank God."

"But give these men a chance, Angie. They're clearly all smitten with you."

"The only one smitten with me is Frank. The others could not care less, and they're probably wondering why they're here." Her nerves skittered. "God, you didn't tell them, did you?"

"No, of course not. I would never violate your privacy like that."

"I almost wish Harper hadn't found the codicil. Then I'd be disinherited and that would be that. Now I have to go through this 'try to find a husband in two months' routine. It's humiliating."

"I know, honey. I'm so sorry. I hope you know that your father had absolutely no knowledge of that provision in his grandpa's will. You know he'd never do this to you."

She shook her head, her hands on her hips. "He was about to disinherit me himself." Then she softened. "I'm sorry, Mama. I know he never meant it. He told me on his deathbed. He never would have gone through with it."

"No, he wouldn't have," her mother said. "You were his pride and joy, Angelina. His mother's namesake. He couldn't have loved you more if—"

Why did she stop? "If what, Mama?"

Maria smiled and shook her head. "Nothing. Nothing at all." She urged Angie back out to the living room. "You mustn't be a poor hostess. Go out there and shine."

Shine? These shoes hurt like hell, and the dress that had fit like a glove in the store was now too tight. But shine she would. She pasted a smile on her face and returned to the sea of men.

★ ★ ★

"Annie, I owe you one," Rafe said at the door of Annie and Dallas McCray's ranch house.

"You and Tom are great tenants and friends," the pretty curly-haired woman said. "Dallas is happy to help."

"How are you feeling?"

"Just a little queasy and hot-flashy, same as last time. The doc says that means everything's good. Come on in. Dallas is in the kitchen."

Rafe followed Annie through the living area to the large kitchen in the back.

"Dallas, you know Rafe."

Dallas stood and stretched out his hand. "Of course. Chad speaks highly of you. I hear you're teaching Angelina Bay how to ride."

No longer. She'd find another instructor. Maybe an instructor who could be her husband. The thought haunted him.

"I'm sorry to interrupt your Sunday morning."

"No problem. The girls are on a day trip to the zoo with their aunt and uncle, so it's just Annie and me today. She tells me you have a legal problem."

"Yes."

"You should know I'm not a practicing attorney. I'm licensed and I know a little, but my work is here on the ranch."

"Yeah, I understand. But I need some guidance, and you seemed the most likely choice. I mean, you're my boss's brother and all, and Annie's my landlord, so I figured I had an in."

Dallas laughed. "You want some coffee? Or herb tea? Annie doesn't drink coffee."

"Coffee would be great, thanks."

"I'll get it, hon," Annie said. "You two go ahead and talk."

Annie poured a cup of coffee and set it on the table. "Come on and sit down."

He sat down and took a sip of the hot brew. Nice and strong, just as he liked it.

"Angelina's brother, Harper, is also a lawyer," Dallas said. "Well, a rancher who's trained as a lawyer, same as me."

Rafe nodded and swallowed another sip of coffee. "I know, but I can't talk to him about this."

"Okay," Dallas said. "So what's up?"

Where to start? "It's a long story."

"Best to start at the beginning then."

"Do you know my father, Jack Grayhawk? He lives over in Echo Gardens?"

"No, can't say I do. He in some kind of trouble?"

"No, nothing like that." He took another sip of coffee and let the strong liquid soothe his parched throat. He hadn't slept at all last night. Sat up inhaling Angie's scent still clinging to his sheets, wondering how he could make this up to her...and knowing there was no way he could.

"My father has a thirty-five-year-old Mexican woman who lives with him. She's been there for about five years, since before my ma died. She cooks and keeps house. Her name is Lilia Martinez."

Dallas nodded. "Okay."

"Lilia—" Rafe closed his eyes and inhaled. "She's my wife."

CHAPTER FIFTEEN

"I didn't know you were married, Rafe," Annie said.

"Well, I'm not. Not really. It's a marriage on paper only."

"Oh?" Dallas said. "What do you mean?"

"Lilia moved to the trailer park about six years ago, and my parents became quite fond of her. She didn't have much money and she rented a room from one of the other residents. She was cleaning houses, but having a hard time making ends meet. When the other residents moved out and sold their trailer, she had no place to go."

"Surely she could find another place to live."

"She wasn't making enough cleaning houses to find her own place."

"Then why didn't she get a different job?"

"She... She couldn't. She didn't have a green card and she couldn't get one."

Annie touched Rafe's forearm in a motherly way. "Was she here illegally?"

"No. At least, not at the beginning." Rafe inhaled. Time to pay the piper. "Her visa had expired."

"So she came here legally?" Dallas said. "At least originally?"

"Yeah. Some friends helped her get the necessary documents and leave before her father and brother found out."

"I see." Dallas drummed his fingers on the table. "So she has a valid Mexican passport?"

"As far as I know, yes."

"And what type of visa did she carry?"

"She was in a hurry, and the quickest way to get a visa was for study abroad here in the U.S."

"Did she actually study?"

"She planned to."

"But she didn't."

"Not that I know of. She was supposed to meet relatives here in Colorado who would help her get registered at school. She was supposed to live with them."

"Let me guess. The relatives never surfaced."

"Right. She was naïve, no doubt. But at least she was away from her past."

"Oh?"

"Her father and brother were heads of a big drug ring in Nogales. She'd suffered from their abuse for years. She'd finally escaped about three months before she showed up in our trailer park, looking for relatives she couldn't find. She'd made her way here by working odd jobs as much as she could, getting paid in cash. One of the families, Thompson was their name, at Echo Gardens took her in. She kept their house and did other house cleaning jobs. When they sold their trailer a few months later and moved on, they didn't take her with them."

"So she didn't go to school, and her visa expired a year later."

"And there were no relatives?" Annie said.

"None that she ever found."

"Once her visa expired, she was here illegally. She needed work, and she couldn't go back to Nogales, face her brother and father, and return to the abuse. She told my mother things—things she wouldn't repeat to my father or me. My mother just cried and said we had to protect Lilia no matter what."

"I see," Dallas said, "so that's how you ended up marrying her?"

"Like I said, my parents were really fond of her. They couldn't let her be deported. I was the only option."

"What about Tom?" Annie asked.

"Tom was already married. They got divorced two years later."

Rafe paused, but neither Dallas nor Annie spoke.

"She needed to be able to work. She needed a green card. By marrying a U.S. citizen, she was able to get one."

"I see," Dallas said again. "This may be none of my business, but did you have any feelings for her at all?"

"I was fond of her. She was kind of like a big sister to me."

"No feelings of love?"

"Sure, I loved her. But not in a sexual way."

Dallas let out a slow breath. "I'm not judging you, but you realize you broke the law, right?"

Rafe nodded. "I know it seems ridiculous. It does to me too. But at the time, I was twenty years old. I swore I'd never marry, never want kids. It was a stupid decision."

"It wasn't stupid to want to protect an innocent woman," Annie said.

"No. I have no regrets about helping Lilia. Neither my parents nor I liked the idea of breaking the law, though."

"I guess I can understand that." Dallas stood. "So what do you need me for?"

"Simple," Rafe said. "I want a divorce."

★ ★ ★

Mrs. Franklin John Longhorn.

She gulped as her esophagus threatened to reverse. The sound of it nauseated her.

All her kids' ears would stick out.

But she'd have her inheritance, along with all Frank's money. No problem with her shopping habits. She didn't have to learn to ranch after all.

And no more riding lessons with Rafe Grayhawk...

She'd have to sleep with Frank. Let him kiss her, touch her, probe her most intimate parts.

She shook her head to clear it. Mama was right. There was no other way. Besides, Frank adored her. He always had. He'd broken out in tears when she'd gotten engaged to Zach McCray all those years ago.

She held her head high as she walked into Deb's Boutique.

The redheaded pain in the ass approached her. "Hello, Angie."

"Hello, Lori. Is Deb here?"

"I'm sorry, she's not feeling well today. She called me and told me you wanted a private Sunday shopping session and asked me to come in. What can I help you with?"

Angie stood silent for a moment, collecting herself. Was she completely presumptuous expecting Deb to open the store on a Sunday just for her? She'd done it before. Why not now? Why hadn't she just told her she wasn't feeling well when Angie had called? She sighed. She'd give Lori a chance. After all, how difficult could it be to pick out a dress for a small courthouse wedding next Saturday?

★ ★ ★

Dallas cleared his throat. "A divorce."

"Yes."

"May I ask why?"

Rafe fidgeted with the handle of his coffee mug. "I'd like to marry someone else."

"I see." Dallas rose from the table and paced to the kitchen. He picked up the carafe. "More coffee?"

Rafe shook his head as Dallas poured himself a cup, returned to the table, and sat down.

"Is there any way to end this marriage without harming Lilia?"

"I'm not an immigration lawyer." He took a sip of coffee. "Do you think Lilia would be willing to return to Mexico if there was no threat to her?"

"I haven't asked her, but I don't see why she wouldn't."

"Who knows about this marriage?"

"Just my father, Tom, and me. Lilia didn't change her name. Anyone who sees her green card just assumes she's a legal immigrant, which she is, as my wife."

"We could dissolve the marriage quietly," Dallas said. "That's not the issue. The issue is protecting both you and Lilia."

"Yes, I know. We had to go through the interview process when Lilia got her green card. We played the loving couple, and the officer who interviewed us didn't look twice. He knew the situation, that she was here on a student visa that was about to expire, and that we'd decided to get married so she didn't need to renew her visa. And it's not like she got something for nothing. She pays her taxes like everyone else."

"True, and that will no doubt be considered." He sipped again. "Is there anyone else who might be willing to marry her if you divorce her?"

"She keeps a low profile. She hasn't dated, to my knowledge. She seems perfectly happy keeping house for my father in that little trailer."

"I don't think there would be any harm to Lilia. Since she's been married to you for more than three years, her resident status probably won't change."

Rafe breathed out in relief. "That's good news then."

"Yes, but like I said, I'm not an immigration attorney. We really need to run this by someone who knows the current laws."

"Do you know anyone?"

"Of course. I know several people in Denver who could take a look. Some who owe me favors."

"How much would that cost?"

Dallas smiled. "For you? Nothing. Like I said, they owe me favors."

Rafe widened his eyes. "Really? That'd be wonderful. I never expected to get anything for nothing."

"I know that. But if Annie and Chad both vouch for you, I have no problem trading in a favor for you. Give me a day or two, and let me see what I can come up with."

"Great!" Rafe nearly jumped out of his skin. "If everything works out, how soon can I get the divorce?"

"Not sure on that one. You don't have any property to split, no children. Should be pretty straightforward. I'd say you could be a free man in six months."

Six months? Angie needed him in two months.

"Can we speed that up a little?"

"Not in this state. You have to wait ninety days after papers are served. You could go to Las Vegas, but one of you would have to live there for six weeks to establish residency."

"Crap." Rafe sighed. What was the point now? He couldn't save Angie's ranch. No doubt she wouldn't have him.

"What's the hurry, if you don't mind my asking?"

"This is all confidential, right?"

"Absolutely."

"Do you want me to leave, Rafe?" Annie asked.

"No, of course not. Please stay."

In a daze, he poured out the story of Angie and her long lost uncle. "I don't know everything, but that's the gist of it, to my understanding."

"I feel for Angie, Rafe, I really do," Annie said, "but do you really want to get into another marriage for the wrong reasons?"

"I have to agree with my wife," Dallas said. "Marrying for any reason other than true love is not the way to go. Trust me, I've been there and I know."

Rafe nodded, his mind racing. Why did he want to marry her? Was it solely to help her? To save her inheritance?

No.

I love her.

He loved Angelina Bay.

Or rather, he loved the Angie he knew when they were alone. The woman who bought clothes like they were penny candy? Not so much.

But they were the same woman. One and the same. How could he love one but not the other?

He couldn't. *I love them both. I love her.*

"Is it possible there was a loophole in the grandfather's

will?" Annie asked.

"If there was," Dallas said, "Harper would have found it."

"Like I said, I don't know the whole story." Rafe stood. "I've taken up enough of your time. Thanks so much to both of you."

Dallas stood and shook his hand. "I'll call in that favor first thing tomorrow morning, bright and early. I'll call you when I have any information."

"I'm obliged," Rafe said.

When he'd shut the front door of the ranch house behind him, his cell phone buzzed.

Tom. "Yeah, Tom, what's up?"

"Come to the doc's," Tom said. "It's Dad."

CHAPTER SIXTEEN

"What happened?" Rafe asked Tom as he hurried into Doc Larson's office.

"He's back getting an x-ray. Called the doc in on his day off."

"Well, that's the chance you take being a small-town doc."

"True that. He fell getting out of the tub. That darn hip of his."

"Where's Lilia?"

"Around the corner getting us some coffees from Rena's. You want anything?" He held up his phone. "I can call her."

"No, no, I just had some coffee. I'm good."

"Good news," Doc said as he entered the waiting room. "No fracture. Just some bruised ribs. He'll be in some pain, but he'll be good as new in a few weeks. I'll give him a couple Percocet. After that ibuprofen should be fine."

Lilia came in with the coffees. She handed one to Tom and one to Doc. "How is he?"

Doc smiled. "He'll be fine. Nothing's broken, just bruised."

"Thank God." Lilia sat down. "I was so worried. He's so stubborn sometimes. He scares the devil out of me when he insists on going out walking alone at night. I'm always afraid he'll fall and hurt himself. And then he falls getting out of the tub!"

Tom laughed. "At least he's keeping clean."

"It's not funny. If anything happened to him—"

"Nothing's going to happen to him," Rafe said. "Like you said, he's too stubborn to let anything truly bad happen. If he'd use a cane, his life would be a little easier, but he's too stubborn."

"Too proud," Tom said.

"Proud, schmoud," Lilia said. "He's still young at heart. Still handsome as anything. So his hips don't work like they used to. So what?"

"We're sure glad he has you around, Lilia," Tom said.

Yeah, Lilia was a godsend. And here he was screwing everything up. What if she had to go back to Mexico? What would his father do? Rafe and Tom would have to step up and pick up the slack, that was all. They'd get him a housekeeper. It would cut into the money for the Arizona place, but so be it.

Unless...

No. Even if he couldn't help Angie, he still needed to dissolve his marriage. Both he and Lilia deserved better than a marriage on paper only. They deserved love.

"He doesn't listen. Tells me I'm nagging." Lilia took a tissue out of her purse, wiped at her eyes, and blew her nose. "Well, maybe I am nagging, but it's for his own good."

Tom laughed out loud. "You sound just like our mother."

Rafe agreed. "He hated her nagging. He's always been stubborn. Never did know what was good for him."

A few minutes later, out came Jack Grayhawk, leaning on Doc Larson.

"I taped him up real good," Doc said. "Leave him taped up for twenty-four hours. Here's four Percocet. Take one every six hours, Jack."

"I don't need any drugs."

"You stubborn man." Lilia shook her finger at him. "You'll

do what the doc says."

Rafe chuckled. Yep, just like Ma used to say. Maybe Lilia would have better luck. He doubted it.

"You boys go on home," Jack said. "It'll take more than a little fall to bring me down."

"Just promise you'll be a little more careful, Dad," Rafe said, as he and Tom each took one arm.

"Oh, he will be," Lilia said. "The boys'll get you into the car. Let's get you home."

They helped him into the passenger side of his car while Lilia sat down in the driver's seat. Soon Rafe's father was heading toward Echo Gardens.

"Hey"—Tom pointed—"isn't that your girlfriend?"

Rafe shifted his gaze. Angelina Bay was leaving the boutique, her arms full of packages. What was the boutique doing open on a Sunday?

"She's not my girlfriend." *But God, I wish she were.*

"Sure seemed that way the other night at the bar. I was afraid you two were going to make a baby right there on the dance floor."

Yes, they had gotten carried away. The fresh lavender scent of her hair still made his nostrils tingle, the smoky orange taste of her kisses, her soft breasts crushed against him as they swayed to the music.

But that was all over now. He couldn't marry her in time to save her ranch. So what good was he? She didn't want him any longer anyway. She wouldn't even listen to him when he'd tried to explain about his marriage.

And she'd never said she loved him.

He was nothing. Just a ranch hand. She'd made that clear as day.

So why can't I get her out of my heart?

"Hey there!" Tom gestured to Angie.

"Shit. Don't call her over here."

"Too late."

Angie ambled over, her bags an obvious burden.

"Let us help you with those," Tom said, taking the biggest one and handing it to Rafe. "Here, help the lady to her car."

Rafe gave his brother what he hoped was a "fuck you" look.

Tom laughed. "I gotta run. An...appointment."

"On Sunday?" Rafe tried the "fuck you" look again.

"Yep, on Sunday. See you." With a tip of his hat, he was gone.

I owe you one, Tom.

"What are you doing around here today?" Angie asked.

"I live just down the street, as you recall."

"Right." Her cheeks turned crimson.

God, she is beautiful. So damn beautiful. "How about you," he said. "What's going on? Why are you in town on a Sunday?"

"Shopping. Deb opens up special for me when I need her to."

"Oh." Pretentious as all get out. What did he see in her again? "So you had a shopping emergency, is that it?"

"In a manner of speaking," she said. "I needed a wedding dress. I'm getting married on Saturday."

Rafe's whole body quaked. Had someone punched him in the gut? He took a deep breath. "Who's the lucky guy?"

"Frank Longhorn."

"Oh." Longhorn was a rancher about Angelina's age. He had much more to offer her anyway. A woman like her deserved...

What did a woman like her deserve?

A man who wasn't already married, for one.

"Nice choice. He'll be able to afford you."

He regretted the words as soon as he'd uttered them. She dropped her packages by the trunk of her car and fished in her purse.

"You can go now. I'll be fine."

Something primal overtook him then. He seized her, her hand still in her purse, pushed her against the door of her car, and slammed his lips onto hers.

Open damn it! Open your lips for me.

As if she read his mind, she opened. Her sweet tongue darted out and met his. He could kiss her forever and never tire of her unique flavor. Their tongues tangled and mated, their lips slid and mashed together. The kiss was raw, unapologetic, yet still seductive and mind-blowing.

For a millisecond, he tried to capture the moment, ink it on his brain so he could pull it out for sustenance once she was married to someone else.

Someone else.

Someone else in her bed. Touching her beautiful body, kissing her private parts, making love to her...

He deepened his assault on her mouth, his desire becoming a need—a need to possess every part of her. He was a beast in the jungle, and she his mate.

When his ferocity melted a little, the kiss become more tender, more loving. Loving. Yes. He'd been right before. He loved this woman. Never had a mere kiss been so meaningful, so much like the actual act of making love.

He broke the suction of their mouths and rained tiny kisses along her cheeks, the sexy curve of her neck. Oh, he could live forever on her and only her. If only he could have said yes when she asked him to marry her. If only...

"Rafe," she said against his cheek, her breath a soft whisper against this skin.

"Baby, come home with me."

"God, Rafe." She nibbled on his earlobe, her soft puffs tickling the inside of his ear.

"Please. Come to my bed. Let me make love to you."

She ran her tongue along the outer edge of his ear. Damn, she made him crazy.

"Please, baby. Please. I need you."

His erection pulsed inside his jeans. An orgasm threatened to erupt...from a kiss. He steeled himself, willed his desire to wane. Didn't work. He needed her. In his bed. In his life. In his heart.

She'd never be out of his heart.

In an instant, she pushed him away, still panting. His dick throbbed, aching for her fingers, her tongue.

"Baby?"

She closed her eyes, sniffed. "I can't. I'm promised to someone else." Quickly she plucked her packages off the ground, opened her car door, and threw them in. "Goodbye, Rafe."

Averting her gaze, she got into the car and drove off.

Off to marry another man, so she could keep her ranch.

Angie Bay, who valued things over people, property over—

Over what? True, he loved her, but she'd never said she loved him. Maybe she didn't value property over love. Maybe she didn't value love at all. Maybe she was incapable of the emotion.

He shook his head. No. Couldn't be. Not the way she kissed him, touched him, made love to him. She had to be capable of something other than greed. That, or she was one mighty fine actress.

His mind tumbled to the packages of clothes she didn't need.

Actress it is.

★ ★ ★

"Thanks for coming over," Dallas said, opening the door on Tuesday. "There's someone here I'd like you to meet."

Rafe walked in. "Where's Annie?"

"At the clinic. Didn't you see her when you left?"

"Nope, she wasn't in yet."

"Good thing. She had the girls with her. You know how they love you."

"They're great kids," Rafe said. And they were. Twin girls, Laurie and Sylvie, who looked exactly like their daddy. What he wouldn't give for a bronze-skinned little girl with Angie's emerald eyes.

But that wasn't to be.

Dallas led him into the kitchen where they'd talked previously. "This is my friend Lisa Cohn. She's an immigration lawyer."

Right. Dallas had promised to call in a favor for him. Too bad he no longer needed it. Since Angie was marrying someone else, no reason existed to dissolve his marriage to Lilia after all. Yes, they both deserved love, but there was no hurry now. Everything could continue as planned. Course Dallas had gone to a lot of trouble. He might as well hear the lady out.

"Nice to meet you," Rafe said.

Lisa stood. "You too. Dallas and Annie speak highly of

you."

"I appreciate that."

"Sit, please."

He sat.

"Dallas told me a little about your situation. I looked into your file. Obviously you passed the interview five years ago."

"Yes, we did fine."

"First of all, you broke the law. You know that. But it was a noble thing you did. Lilia Martinez is the daughter of the biggest drug lord in Nogales, right on the border."

"Yes, I know."

"Life couldn't have been easy for her. Do you know any of her circumstances?"

"Just that she was physically and emotionally abused by her father and her brother. She told my mother things, things she'd never repeat to us. All she'd say is we didn't know the half of it, and Lilia had sworn her to secrecy. She said we had to protect Lilia, that her life depended on it. Those secrets died with my mother."

Lisa nodded. "I can understand why you married her to protect her. It's skating around the law, but sometimes there's good reason." She cleared her throat. "The good thing is, Lilia didn't enter the U.S. illegally. She had a valid student visa. So that's in your favor. I'm pretty sure I can fix it so she can keep her green card since you've been married for over three years."

Great. Didn't matter now, but whatever. "That's kind of you."

Lisa took a sip from the glass of water in front of her. "Is Lilia involved with anyone?"

"Why would that matter?"

"Because if she could marry someone else, it would help.

But it's not a necessity."

Rafe rubbed his eyes. Such a long couple of days. "Honestly, I don't know. She seems happy just working for the realtor and keeping house for my dad. She's really a great person."

"I'm sure she is." Lisa shuffled some papers on the table. "Here are the forms you need to file to dissolve your marriage. Only one of you needs to file, and since you're here, let's go ahead and get this ball rolling."

A lump formed in Rafe's throat. He hadn't even talked to Lilia about this. And now? With Angie marrying someone else? He didn't need to go through with this at all.

He sighed. Wrong. It was time. Angie was marrying a man she didn't love. Rafe—and Lilia—deserved better than that. Once their marriage was dissolved, they could each find love and spend eternity wed to their soul mates.

Well, at least Lilia could. Rafe had already found love. Too bad it would never be returned. Maybe though, just maybe, he'd find it again someday.

He signed on the dotted line and shook hands with Lisa and Dallas. "Thank you for your generosity and kindness. Both of you."

"You're most welcome," Lisa said. "I'll be in touch."

Rafe said goodbye and left.

Now home, to tell Lilia they were getting a divorce.

CHAPTER SEVENTEEN

"How did you get him to start using that cane?" Rafe asked Lilia.

"I finally put my foot down." Her smile gleamed. She looked as though she'd just conquered Mount Everest. "I told him I was out of here if he didn't start taking better care of himself."

Her soft gaze rested on his father. Was that love in her eyes? Rafe wasn't sure. He inhaled and let out the air in a slow stream. Now or never.

"I need to talk to you two."

"About what, son?"

"About...us, I guess. Lilia and me." He cleared his throat. "I think it's time to end the marriage."

Lilia and his father looked at each other. Neither seemed fazed. What was going on?

His father lifted his gaze to Rafe. "Could I ask why?"

"I've...been thinking. A lot, actually. I was young when I agreed to this, and at the time I didn't think I'd ever want to marry or have kids. I've changed my mind."

"Oh," Jack said.

"But don't worry. I've talked to a lawyer, and Lilia will be able to keep her green card since we were married more than three years. It's all worked out."

"How much will it cost?" Lilia asked.

"The filing fees, of course. Other than that, nothing. I'll

owe Dallas McCray a big favor, but nothing, for now." He grinned. "Maybe I can give his kids riding lessons or something. I'll figure it out."

"I don't like you beholden to anyone, boy," Jack said. "We Grayhawks find our own way."

"Finding our own way sometimes means accepting help when it's offered," Rafe said. "Then we help others in return."

"He's right, Jack," Lilia said. "If I hadn't accepted help from your family, where would I be today?" She smiled. "Besides, it'll solve our little problem."

Rafe widened his eyes. "What problem would that be?"

"Come here, honey," Jack said to Lilia, and she went to him and perched on his good knee.

Ah, so that's how it is.

"We've fallen in love, son," Jack said. "It's been coming for some time. So Lilia won't have to worry about keeping her green card, because as soon as your marriage is dissolved, I plan to make an honest woman out of her."

"That's wonderful." Rafe's heart warmed. He couldn't have asked for this to work out any better. "I'm happy for both of you."

"What about you?" Jack asked. "Is there a lady in your life? Why this sudden interest in making yourself available?"

Angie's image appeared in Rafe's mind. Beautiful Angie, who kissed him like a temptress and made his knees weak with a mere look. Lovely Angie. *Engaged Angie.*

"Not at the moment," he said.

"What about that Angelina Bay? Tom and that pretty Amber sure tried hard to keep me from seeing you on the dance floor with her."

Rafe laughed. Nothing got past his father. "Angie is a

remarkable woman," Rafe said. "But she's too old for me."

"Age ain't nothin' but a number." Jack gazed at the woman in his lap. "Right, honey?"

"Right," she agreed.

Rafe sighed. "No matter what her age, she can't be mine. She belongs to someone else."

"Oh." Jack's eyes drooped a little. "I just thought—I mean the two of you looked so—"

Rafe simply shook his head.

"I'm sorry, son."

"It's okay. We're from two different worlds, anyway. But my woman's out there somewhere. In the meantime, I'm glad you found yours." He meant those words with his whole heart.

As he left to go back to town, he wondered if he'd ever find his own.

He had a sneaking suspicion he'd already found her.

Too bad she'd never be his.

* * *

"What are you doing here?"

Rafe's deep timbre voice cut through Angie like a saw through a giant redwood. She swallowed. "I still need to learn to ride, don't I? I'm going to be a rancher's wife. You'll still be paid the price we agreed upon." She smoothed Belle's mane. "Besides, my horse is here."

Rafe grabbed the bandana out of his pocket and wiped his face. "I figured our lessons were over. You haven't been here in a while."

"I've had other things to do, as you know. My father just died."

"Yes, I know." He put the handkerchief back in his pocket. "But aren't you getting married day after tomorrow?"

She swallowed again. The thought nauseated her. "Yes. So it's safe to say I won't be here for a lesson tomorrow. I am, however, here today."

"I'm sorry. You're right. We have a deal. Go ahead and bring her out."

Rafe saddled Adonis, and they led the horses to the practice area once again. He helped her mount.

"You obviously did fine with walking and trotting the other day."

"Yes, but I used the reins."

"I know. We'll work on getting you to use your body more so you aren't in her mouth so much. Go ahead and do the circles I taught you last time, only this time, don't hold onto the reins at all."

"At all?" Fear gripped her. Silly, she knew. She'd hardly used the reins the last lesson. Still, they were kind of a security blanket.

"Don't be frightened. I'm right here. I won't let anything happen."

His voice soothed her like a cup of steaming chamomile. As though it could take all the bad away and keep her safe forever.

But it couldn't. Rafe couldn't.

At least she could have him for riding lessons. Spending this small amount of time with him might get her through the next few days. She hoped, anyway.

He'd stopped trying to explain about his marriage. At this point, it didn't matter. He couldn't save her ranch for her, so she'd marry someone else and live without love. It had worked for her parents. They'd grown fond of each other, and they'd respected each other. They'd had two more children, and she knew her mother had suffered several miscarriages between Harper and Catie—one of the reasons they were nine years apart. So sex had worked between them. They no doubt enjoyed it. Sex was fun with anyone, right? She'd enjoyed it with Zach McCray and with others.

But she'd been attracted to everyone she'd had sex with. She was not attracted to Frank Longhorn. He was a nice guy. A genuine guy. A man who genuinely adored her.

More than she could say for the magnificent man with her now.

Why, oh why, does he have to be married? And why, oh why, didn't he tell me before we...

She shook her head. No use ruminating. She'd done herself a disservice coming here today. She'd only prolonged her agony.

Today would be her last riding lesson. Her last riding lesson with Rafe, at least. She'd still learn to ride. She'd promised her daddy, and she meant to keep that promise. She'd be a rancher's wife, after all.

Rafe worked both her and Belle hard, and by the end of the long lesson, her thighs and buttocks were sore and miserable.

"I'm going over to Catie's pool and sit in the hot tub," she said.

"Okay, have a nice time."

"Want to come?" she blurted out before she could stop herself. *Damn. Not the way to fall out of love Rafe Grayhawk.*

"I'm on the clock, sorry."

"Yes, of course. I know that. But...Chad took Catie into Denver for a pregnancy checkup."

"Wish I could. Can't."

"I understand."

He nodded. "Go ahead and get Belle situated. I'll see you Monday for your lesson, I guess. By then you'll be Mrs. Longhorn."

She shook her head. "I won't be coming back. This will be my last lesson."

"Thought you said you needed to learn to ride. You being a rancher's wife and all."

"True. I will need lessons. But I'll find someone else. Seeing you...it's too..." Too what? Too hard? Too sad? Too much like stabbing herself in the heart?

All of the above.

"You interested in hearing me out yet?"

She shook her head. "What would be the point? I'm marrying Frank. I have to."

"Damn it, Angie, you don't *have* to do anything."

"You don't understand. I can't lose my ranch. I just can't. I don't have anything else."

"You'd have—" He stopped.

"What?"

"Never mind. Enjoy your dip." He tipped his hat, removed it, and wiped his face. "On second thought, I might just join you after all. Chad always says the pool is at our disposal if we need it, long as we warn Catie we're comin'. Since she's not home, I guess that rule doesn't apply."

Her heart leaped. He'd come with her. She recalled their previous time at the pool when he'd driven her crazy and then left. How she'd hungered for him to finish what he started. And finished he had, the next day.

They didn't talk as they tended the horses, and then made

their way to the pool house. Angie's nipples were straining against her bra by the time they got there. Rafe's arousal was evident beneath his jeans.

Such a beautiful man. With such a beautiful body. Even his golden bronze cock was beautiful.

Would Frank's be beautiful?

Shivers raced down her spine. She didn't want to find out. Why was she thinking about him anyway? She'd enjoy this last hurrah with Rafe. It was just a date in the pool and hot tub after all. Nothing dishonest about that.

He'd left her in the pool house to change. She grabbed her red bikini off the hook and undressed.

Why did she need the bikini? It's not like that hadn't seen each other naked before. And no one was home. Chad and Catie would be gone all day...

She hung the suit back on the hook and stepped out of the pool house buck naked.

Rafe's eyes turned to dinner plates.

Good, good. Just what I wanted. "I figured you wouldn't have a suit here, so I didn't want to make you feel bad."

"God, baby. Why are you doing this?"

"Doing what?" Good, let him squirm. Let him see what he'd be missing. Let him imagine her using her body to pleasure Frank Longhorn in bed.

He stalked toward her like a wolf scenting his mate. "Damn you." He grabbed her and pulled her to him, crushing her body to his.

Their lips met in a frenzy of teeth and tongues.

She gasped, her heart beating so hard against her chest she knew he must be able to feel it. "You have too many clothes on."

"Damn right I do." He shed them quickly.

Her skin tingled as he bared himself. So gorgeous, a sculptor's dream. A painter's fantasy. Though she had no artistic talent, Angie was sure Rafe could inspire her to create a masterpiece.

She dropped to her knees, the cement of the pool deck grating into her skin. She didn't care. She needed that beautiful cock in her mouth.

Sweet, stiff hardness. She licked the head, sucked on it, trailed tiny kisses down to the base of his shaft.

"God, baby." His voice cracked.

"Mmm, you like?" she teased.

"I like." He grabbed the back of her head. "Take me. Take all of me."

She obliged, taking as much of him as she could into her mouth. Pleasure ripped through her. He stroked her hair, keeping to her rhythm, never rushing her, moving with her, guiding her in his pleasure. Giving oral had never been her favorite part of sex. Rafe changed that.

"Baby, baby, yes, yes." His voice drifted over her, a soothing caress.

No man had ever ejaculated in her mouth. She'd never even considered it, thought it too...too... She wasn't sure. But she was sure right now. She wanted that from Rafe.

She continued to torment him, adding her hands so she could pleasure his entire massive length at once.

"Baby, slow down. I don't want to... God, slow down."

Not in this lifetime. She wanted this more than she wanted to breathe. She continued her assault, faster, faster, faster...

Until pulses began beneath her tongue.

"God, baby, I can't stop it—" He panted, his breath coming

in rapid gasps.

She continued, hoping he knew it was okay. Hoping he would give her this gift that she'd treasure always. Hoping—

He came with a gush over her tongue. The salty tang of him slid over the roof of her mouth, down her throat.

She shivered. This was the most erotic experience of her life. She'd never forget it.

Never.

And she knew in the depths of her being, she'd do this for no other man. Ever.

She pulled away from him. Rafe's gaze was upon her, staring down at her with lust and anticipation.

"I'm sorry, baby."

She shook her head and smiled, only now realizing the pain in her knees. "Don't be. I wanted it. I wanted to do that for you."

"It was amazing."

"For me too."

He pulled her to him. "I hope you don't think we're done."

"You mean?"

"Hell, yes. I may not be eighteen anymore, but you affect me like no other woman. Let's go sit in that tub and soothe your sore muscles, and I'll show you exactly what I'm capable of."

She couldn't wait.

CHAPTER EIGHTEEN

After a soak, Rafe set Angie on the edge of the tub and tantalized her with his talented tongue. She shivered as he pleasured her, whispered against her flesh how good she tasted, how pretty she was. How would she live without this?

She had to. She had no other choice.

After he had given her several orgasms, he stood and thrust into her. She stared into his black eyes, her gaze never wavering, and dug her nails into his dark shoulders, her back arching, as he pushed into her again and again. Completion, total fulfillment.

Perfection.

"Baby, you feel so good."

Thrust.

Thrust.

Thrust.

"God, so good."

One final thrust, and his cock spasmed inside her. Filling her. Completing her. Making her whole.

He sank against her, his slick chest tantalizing her nipples, and then pulled her back into the water and crushed her against him. Their lips met in a gentle kiss, a soothing kiss.

A kiss that said goodbye.

She held back her tears until he was gone.

★ ★ ★

"Please? Isn't there anything you can do?"

"I'm sorry, Rafe," Lisa said on the other end of the phone. "It's like Dallas said. A divorce takes about six months to finalize. I wish I could help you, but I can't."

"I understand. Thanks." He hung up the phone.

What did it matter anyway? Angie had already decided what was important. Her inheritance. She'd marry a man she didn't love to get it. She'd already made that choice. The fact that they ignited fires in bed didn't matter. The fact that he was hopelessly in love with her didn't matter.

Did she love him? She hadn't said it, and he had no idea.

But their lovemaking was so full of passion, almost surreal. He'd never experienced anything like it.

He feared he never would again.

★ ★ ★

Angie awoke in a cold, clammy sweat. She'd dreamed of Rafe. Of their lovemaking. Of a future with him.

A future with him wasn't possible. He was married to someone else. But perhaps somewhere, she had no idea where, another man existed whom she could love and who could love her in return.

Her parents hadn't been in love. They'd married because Mama had been pregnant with her. While they had given her a wonderful life and she appreciated it more than she could ever say, hadn't they deserved to be in love? Hadn't they deserved to feel about someone the way she felt about Rafe? And hopefully would feel about another man at some point?

One thing had become clear as day.

She could not marry Frank Longhorn.

Her heart broke at losing her inheritance, but it wasn't worth it. The old Angelina would have done anything for the ranch.

Not *this* Angelina.

Not the Angelina who had experienced what it felt like to love another human being with her entire heart and soul.

Before she changed her mind, she called her mother.

"I'm sorry, Mama. I just can't do it. It's not fair to Frank, and it's not fair to me."

"Are you sure, Angelina?"

"Yes, I'm sure. Frank deserves a woman who loves him. A woman who isn't marrying him just to use him. A couple years ago I might have been able to do this, but now I can't. I've changed. I'm not the spoiled brat I used to be."

"I'm proud of you, Angie," her mother said. "And you are right. Frank deserves better. And may God forgive me. Your father deserved better. Most importantly, *you* deserve better. You deserve love. I don't want you to settle for anything less." She sighed. "There may be a way out of this yet. I need to talk to Jefferson."

"I'll come with you."

"Angelina—"

"Mama, this concerns me. Anything you have to say to him can be said in front of me."

"Yes, perhaps it's time."

"Time for what?"

"I'll be at your place in half an hour. Let's go see your uncle."

★ ★ ★

"Mia, and the lovely Angelina." Jefferson Bay's deep voice was laced with sarcasm as he opened the door to his hotel room.

"We need to talk," Maria said.

"Perhaps you and I had best talk in private."

Maria shook her head. "This is Angie's business. After all, she's the one who's about to lose her inheritance."

"So you didn't find a suitable suitor after all?" He clicked his tongue. "How very sad. But how very lucky for me. I now own half a ranch."

"You don't own anything yet, Jeff," Maria said, her voice shaking. "Angie still has over a month to get married."

"Let me guess... She's holding out for love, right? Love is overrated."

"Is it?" Maria inched closer to him. "Is it really? Don't you remember?"

"I remember only that you betrayed me by sleeping with my sainted brother. I may have loved you, but you didn't return my love."

Maria's eyes misted. "That's not true, Jeff. You know it's not."

Dear Lord. Mama and Daddy had never been in true love. They'd made no bones about that. Yet they'd had a good life. All that time, had Mama been in love with someone else? With Jefferson? Angie's legs wobbled beneath her. What else would be revealed today?

"I know only your betrayal, Mia. You slept with my brother and had his child—this beautiful girl in front of us. It's only fitting that I be the means to the end of your and Wayne's love child."

"Damn it, Jeff, you know I was never in love with Wayne."

"Really?" He scoffed. "A marriage that lasted this long and produced three children? You're lying."

"You were going to prison."

"I was innocent! I would have fought, Mia, if I'd thought there was even a ghost of a chance that you and I could be together."

"Why didn't you?"

He raked his fingers through his hair, making it stand on end. A wolf, Angie thought. *He looks like a wolf in fear for his life.* Strange.

"Because you made it clear you thought I was guilty. Dear Granddad had all but hanged me already."

"Why didn't you tell me you were innocent? I would have believed you. I would have stood by you."

"No, you wouldn't have. You had already run to Wayne by then."

"I ran to Wayne because—" She choked into sobs. "My God, I can't do this."

Angie regained the strength in her legs. Her mother needed her. She walked to the woman who had given her life and embraced her. "She just lost her husband, for God's sake. Can't you take it easy on her? I'm the one you're trying to ruin. Your argument is with me, not her."

"How little you know. You've told your children nothing of me, have you, Mia? Yet you stand there and tell me you had feelings for me all that time ago." He glared at Angie. "I can hurt your lovely mother by hurting you. Icing on the cake."

"No, Jeff," Maria choked out. "I won't let you do this to her."

He smiled. Not a nice smile. A wicked smile. An evil smile. "I don't see that you have much of a choice."

"I'm sorry, Mama. I've already told you I'm not marrying Frank. And there isn't time for me to fall in love." She was already in love, but her mother didn't need to know that. It hurt too much to talk about anyway.

Again the blurry vision of Rafe's supposed wife invaded her mind. What might her face look like? Was she brunette like Angie? Or blond? Or red-haired like that horrible Lori at Deb's?

She shook her head. Lori and Deb. She'd been awful to them. Absolutely bratty. Lori wasn't horrible. *Angie* was.

No longer. Along with disinherited Angie came new and improved Angie. She'd make amends for all the nastiness she'd spewed in the past if it took the rest of her life. She'd begin tomorrow by boxing up all the clothes she never needed in the first place and donating them to charity. She'd be moving in with Mama soon anyway. The smaller closet in her old bedroom would thank her.

"You're right, Angie." Maria steadied herself, taking some of her weight off Angie. "You're not going to marry Frank. You're not going to marry anyone you don't love just to get a piece of land."

"Then I think we're done here," Jeff said, moving toward the door. "Nice to see you, ladies."

Maria rushed forward and pounded her fists onto Jeff's chest. "Damn it, Jeff, we are not done here!"

"Mama?" Angie said, inching toward her mother and uncle.

"You won't do this to her. I swear you won't!"

Jefferson gripped her mother's shoulders. "I stand to gain

everything by doing this."

"But you can't."

"You keep saying that, Mia." He shook her.

Angie inched forward a little more. She would not let him hurt her mother. He eased off, though his hands were still clamped onto Maria. Angie inhaled and stayed put.

"Why? Why can't I?" he continued. "Why shouldn't I take what should have been rightfully mine in the first place?"

Maria whipped her hands upward and grabbed both sides of Jefferson's face.

"Because she's *your* daughter, God damn it!"

CHAPTER NINETEEN

Angie's heart plummeted to her stomach. Had she heard right?

"Mama?" Her voice squeaked.

"I'm sorry, Angelina. I shouldn't have blurted it out like that, but it's true. Wayne Bay is not your biological father. Jefferson Bay is."

She swayed, her muscles tensing. Her knees weakened and threatened to collapse under her. Her doting daddy not her daddy? It couldn't be.

"You're lying, Mia," Jefferson said, "and it won't work."

"It's not a lie, you fool. To be honest I'm surprised none of you suspected it at the time. If it's proof you want, you and Angie go for a DNA test. I guarantee the results will show she's yours."

"How? Why?"

"Didn't you wonder why I suddenly had an interest in your brother when I'd had none previously? Didn't you wonder when my baby girl was born a month early? No, none of you gave it a second thought. It seemed so obvious to me, but neither you, Wayne, nor your grandfather batted an eye over it."

The words rang in Angie's ears. First they made sense, and then they didn't, and then she was sure this had to be a dream, and then she knew it wasn't. This was real. Terrible and horrifying and real.

"I think I might be sick," she said.

Maria rushed to her and helped her to one of the queen beds in the hotel room. "I'm so sorry, Angie. I never meant for you to find out like this. I never meant for you to find out at all."

"At all?" Angie blinked her eyes. This *was* her mother, right? The same woman who'd hugged her and kissed her boo boos. The woman who would never keep something this important from her. From her *father*. "How could you? How could you lie to me all these years?"

"I'm sorry."

Sorry? Angie didn't know this woman at all. "Daddy never knew? Never suspected?"

"If he did, I didn't know it."

"Mia, I demand an explanation right now."

Uncle Jefferson. She'd nearly forgotten he was in the room.

"Yes, I owe you both that much." She sat down on the bed and took Angie's hand in her own. She rubbed it lightly. "I found out I was pregnant after you were arrested. With all your trouble with the law, I assumed you were guilty."

"After everything we shared, how could you know me so little? Do you really think I could kill someone?"

"No." Maria shook her head. "But I knew you'd go to prison for a long time anyway. I figured you'd had a hand in it. After all, it wasn't the first time you'd been at the scene of a crime. There was no way around it. You had a record. I needed to make sure my baby—*our* baby—had a chance at the life and the name she deserved. So I seduced Wayne, and a month later, told him the child was his."

Angie's head spun. She widened her eyes, as if toothpicks held her lids up, to keep them open.

Jefferson plunked down onto the other bed. "Oh, Mia."

"I'm not proud of it. But he adored your daughter, Jeff. She was his favorite. She wanted for nothing while he was alive."

"Oh, Mia, you don't understand." His head sank to his hands.

Maria gripped Angie's hand tighter. "What? What are you not telling me?"

"I only pleaded guilty because I thought you'd betrayed me. I'd been ready to fight. To fight for us. To do anything to get out of the mess I'd gotten myself into and go straight for you. I was going to get a job, make my own way, prove to my grandfather that I wasn't the fuck up he thought I was. I was ready to prove it to you. For us. Mia...why?"

Angie gulped back bile. Was this really happening? Images of the words swirled around her head in black-and-gray letters.

"You were the love of my life," Jeff said, his voice wavering. "All this time, I had a child. A child I never knew."

Don't talk about me like I'm not here.

Had she said the words out loud? She wasn't sure.

"Mama?"

"Yes, Angie?"

"Harper and Catie?"

"They're your father's. Er...Wayne's. I never strayed during our marriage. Not once."

"And I—"

"Jeff is your biological father. I'm so sorry. I didn't mean for you to find out this way. Or to find out at all—"

"You planned to keep this child from me forever?" Jeff's voice had deepened, tinted with more anger, almost rage. "Didn't you think I had the right to know I had a child?"

"And didn't you think I had the right to know who my

real father was?" Angie demanded. She tried to sit up, but her vision blurred.

Maria's weight sank down farther into the bed, as though she wanted to melt into it, to melt away and never return. "Angie, you had a real father. A real father who adored you."

She tried opening her eyes again. Bad idea. "Would he have adored me so much if he'd known the truth?"

"I don't know. But what does it matter?"

"What does it matter? Are you serious?"

"And what about me, Mia?" Jeff interjected. "What about me?"

"You were serving a life sentence. What would you have done with a child? What would I have done as a single mother?"

"You never loved Daddy," Angie choked out.

"He never loved me either."

She shook her head, her cheeks rubbing against the too fluffy hotel pillow. "You shouldn't have married him. He deserved to be loved."

Her mother's hand held her own in what felt like a death grip. "I did it for you, Angie. For *you*. Can't anyone see that?"

"Bullshit," Angie said, trying again to rise. She found her strength and sat up. "You did it for yourself. Your boyfriend was going to prison, and you were stuck pregnant. You trapped an innocent man into a marriage neither of you wanted. I'll never forgive you for this. Never!"

"Angie, please."

"The girl's right, Mia. What you did was wrong on so many levels."

Maria sighed. "I'm not arguing that point."

"Christ, Mia. I loved you. I would have done anything for you. For our child."

"You couldn't escape a prison sentence."

"But I would have fought. I could have turned state's evidence, I could have gotten a better lawyer, I could have…"

"I had to make a decision quickly. A decision that I thought was best for my child. You'll be happy to know, Jeff, that Angie never wanted for anything. She had everything a little girl could want."

"Except her real father," Jeff said.

I had a real father.

But he wasn't mine.

He was Harper's.

He was Catie's.

He was never mine.

"You can't take her inheritance. You can't do this to your own daughter."

"She's not my daughter." Jeff stalked forward.

Was he going to grab her mother again?

"You took her from me and gave her to my brother. My sainted brother. He had everything. He was the older. He had Grandpa's love and devotion. He had everything I could never have, except you. I had you. But you took that away and gave yourself to him. You gave my child to him!"

"He wasn't the one I loved, Jeff. You were."

"You think that matters now?"

"Yes, it should matter. The fact that she's yours should matter. Please don't take her ranch away from her."

"The ranch is mine. She can have it when I'm dead. Now the two of you get the hell out of my hotel room." He stormed across the carpet and opened the door.

"Jeff, please."

"Sorry. It's all falling on deaf ears."

"But she's your flesh and blood!"

"She stopped being mine the moment you gave her to Wayne. Now get out!"

Angie's brain was in a fuzzy haze as she leaned on her mother and left her uncle's—her father's—room.

What had just gone on? She wasn't her father's daughter? Her father was her uncle and her uncle was her father? Were her sister and brother her siblings? Or her cousins? Or some twisted hybrid of both?

She didn't have her father. He was dead. She didn't have her inheritance. Her uncle—father—was taking it away. She didn't have a mother anymore. She hated this bitch holding her up. What a liar! She no longer had a fiancé. She'd broken it off with Frank of her own accord. And she didn't have Rafe. He was married to someone else.

Someone else who wasn't her.

She had nothing.

Truly nothing.

Heaviness laced her eyelids. Her mother's brown eyes glared into her own, striking, and then fuzzy, and then striking again. Two Mamas. Then one. Two again. Icy needles pricked at her neck.

The room spun.

A curtain of blackness fell.

★ ★ ★

Angie's eyes fluttered open. Where am I? Her body lay supine on what she thought was a bed. Where am I?

"She's coming to."

Whose voice is that?

Masculine. Deep. Oh, so familiar.

Daddy?

"No, sweetheart. Daddy's gone, remember?"

Had she said that out loud?

Mama?

"Yes, I'm here."

"Where am I?"

"Back in Jeff's hotel room. You fainted after we left. Do you remember?"

Fainted. Daddy. Mama. Uncle Jeff. Her birth father.

Yes, Uncle Jeff was her birth father.

Tears flooded her eyes. Her legs itched. Itched and burned. Move. She needed to move. Had to run. Run far away from these two people. They'd lied to her, cheated her out of her inheritance. They were horrible, ugly people.

Only she couldn't move. Couldn't make her body respond to her need to escape.

What's going on?

"Jeff, maybe we should call 9-1-1."

"Don't be silly. She's fine. She just passed out." His voice got louder. "When's the last time you ate, Angelina?"

Ate? Heck, I have no idea. She hadn't been able to choke down food since Daddy took to the hospital. Then Daddy passed, and Uncle Jeff—Daddy Jeff—showed up and took her inheritance. Scrambled eggs appeared in her brain. Yes, Rafe had fed her a bite of eggs. Then he'd dropped the bomb about being married, she got engaged to Frank, and now she found out her daddy wasn't her daddy after all. Had she truly only eaten scrambled eggs since...since...

"Can you answer, Angie?" her mother asked.

Angie shook her head. "I... I'm not sure."

"I didn't see you eat anything at the memorial service, or at the party we gave for the men." She smoothed Angie's hair off her forehead. "Jeff, I think we need to feed her."

"I'll call room service."

"This is Bakersville. Small-town hotel. There's no room service here."

"Fine, fine." He sighed. "I'll go down and find something for her. Wait here."

The door squeaked lightly as it closed.

"Angie, darling, I'm so sorry," her mother said.

Doesn't matter. I hate you. I hate him. I'll never forgive either of you. Her vocal cords seemed fused. Couldn't bring the words out. She wanted to say them. Lord, how she longed to say them. She had nothing.

Nothing.

"Angie, I hope you can forgive me."

Angie turned her head to look away from her mother's face. She focused on the beige wall of the hotel room.

Icky plain beige.

"All right. I won't force you to talk," Maria said. "We'll wait till Jeff gets back with some food."

You'll be waiting a heck of a lot longer than that. I'm through with you. Through with Uncle Daddy Jeff. Through with men I don't love. Through with the man I do love. Through with everything. What left is there to live for?

Maria smoothed her hair back again, but Angie jerked her head.

Don't touch me.

She closed her eyes. The soft breath of her mother's sigh met her ears.

"I'm so sorry, Angie. This will work out. I promise."

I promise.

Right.

The door squeaked open. "I'm back."

Jeff's voice.

So like her father's...

It *was* her father's...

"I got her a turkey sandwich and some water. Something easy for her stomach."

"Good thinking." Her mother's voice. "Can you sit up. Angie?"

Go away.

"Come on, sit up." Her mother urged her forward, and she leaned back upon several pillows. "You have to eat something, sweetheart. Please."

Her mother unwrapped the sandwich and tore off a piece. "Here."

Angie turned her head away.

"Come on now."

Her stomach betrayed her and growled. Yes, she was hungry. Her tummy felt gaunt and empty, as though she hadn't eaten well in days. Which, of course, she hadn't.

She opened her mouth and took the bite.

"Good girl," Maria said.

She chewed the meat and bread into a tasteless lump and forced it down her throat. And found, to her surprise, that she wanted more. She took the rest of the sandwich from her mother's hand.

"Thank God," Maria said.

"She'll be fine, Mia. She's just hungry."

"For God's sake, Jeff, she's more than hungry. Her father just died. Then you showed up and took her inheritance. What do you expect?"

Jeff said nothing. Or if he did, Angie didn't hear it. She was busy munching on the sandwich.

"Water," she said.

Maria opened the bottle of water and handed it to her. "I know this is all very upsetting, sweetheart. I'm sorry I blurted it out like that." She stood and pulled on her brown hair. "I just didn't know what else to do."

Angie drank the water and said nothing.

"Jeff, please."

"I'm not discussing this anymore, Maria. The child is fine. She's just hungry and probably a little depressed with all that's gone on."

"You could help her, you know."

"No one helped me my entire life."

Maria sighed and moved toward him. "You're never going to change, are you? Always a victim. Nothing is ever your fault. You could have led a better life, you know. You didn't have to be such a rebel."

"You liked me that way. You found it exciting."

"I was eighteen years old, for goodness' sake. Of course I found you exciting. But I grew up, Jeff. The minute I found out I was pregnant I grew up. That baby became the most important thing in my life. Her life was more important than my own, and I made sure I gave her the best I could."

"That's the difference between us, I guess," Jeff said. "You didn't give me the chance to give her a good life."

Uncle Jeff walked out the door again.

Angie finished her water.

"Are you better now? Can you stand up? I want to get you home. I want to get you away from that man."

Angie nodded. She wouldn't forgive her mother, but right now she needed to leave this room as much as Maria did.

She said the words in her mind that now had two distinct meanings.

Goodbye, Daddy.

CHAPTER TWENTY

He had to see her.

Had to see her one more time before she married another man.

Maybe kiss her one more time. Would it be enough to last the rest of his life? Probably not. But he had to tell her how he felt. Yes, it was too late. She'd made that clear. But she deserved to know.

Rafe hopped in his car Saturday morning and sped to Angelina's.

★ ★ ★

Angie picked up her cell phone. "Hi, Catie. What's up?"

Silence on the other end of the line.

"Catie?"

"Ang, listen. Chad and I have been talking."

"Yeah?"

"I want to... That is *we* want to...to give you our share of Bay Crossing."

Angie dropped the phone and picked it up quickly. "What?"

"I'm serious. We don't need it, and we both feel terrible about what your fa—" She coughed. "What Uncle Jefferson is putting you through."

A tempting offer, but one the new Angie would not accept.

"I love you both for offering," she told her sister, "but it's time I made my own way. I don't know anything about ranching yet. I'm staying here with Mama. We have a lot to work out."

"But Ang—"

"I'm going to work things out with her, don't worry. After that, I'll find my way, I promise. You just take care of yourself and that little angel you're carrying."

Catie gulped and said goodbye with a quiet sob.

Her sister and brother-in-law were good people. The best. But she couldn't depend on them or anyone else anymore. Time for Angelina Bay to make it on her own.

She put the phone in her pocket and got back to work folding clothes and placing them in boxes. Later she'd drive into Denver to donate them to one of the shelters. Preferably one for single mothers and their children in need. They held a special place in her heart.

After all, she could have easily been one of those children herself.

When a rapping met her ears, she quickly taped up the box of clothes and got up to answer her door.

Rafe stood on the other side, his hair in his signature ponytail, his jeans slung low on his hips as usual. Sadness shadowed his beautiful bronze features.

"Hello, Rafe."

"May I come in?"

She sighed. Why not? "Sure." She held the door open for him.

He looked around her cluttered living room. "Getting ready to move, I guess?"

She shook her head. "These are actually donations to charity. I went through my closet this morning. I decided I don't need but about a quarter of the clothes I have. So I'm going to help those less fortunate than myself."

He didn't smile. "That's right nice of you, Angie."

"Oh, I don't know how nice it is." She smiled, hoping it didn't look too forced. "I wish I knew more about being nice. But it's never too late to learn, I guess."

Still no smile from Rafe. "The poor will appreciate your sacrifice. And your future husband can buy you a whole new wardrobe, anyway."

She shook her head. He thought she was being facetious. Of course he did. He only had her past actions to consider. Time for him to meet the new Angie.

"No new wardrobe. From now on, I'm only buying what I need."

"Oh?" His eyes widened. "You'll save him a bundle then."

She let out a breathy laugh...or what she hoped sounded like a laugh. "I'll save him more than that. I'm not getting married after all, Rafe. I couldn't go through with it."

His eyebrows rose. "Oh?"

"My parents married for the wrong reasons, and I can't do it. I won't marry unless it's for love. And I can't fall in love in two months."

She couldn't fall in love because she was already in love. In love with a man who was married to someone else. The man standing before her now. But she couldn't tell him that. He'd never know.

In a flash, his demeanor changed. Still no smile, but he grabbed her shoulders and his dark eyes came back to life. "Could you get married if someone loved you?"

"No." She shook her head. "Frank loves me. Or he's at least infatuated with me. He has been for years. But he deserves a woman who loves him."

"Most men do," Rafe said. "And I agree with you. Getting married for the wrong reason, no matter what the circumstances, is a mistake. Believe me, I know." He touched her cheek oh-so-gently. "Angie, would you listen to me? Would you let me tell you about my...my wife?"

His touch seared her. But she steeled her strength against her need for him. "I don't see what purpose that would serve at this point."

"It would serve many purposes, the most important of which is that I want you to know the truth. It's important to me."

She sighed. Fine. What could it hurt? It didn't matter now anyway. She'd lost the ranch. More importantly, she'd lost Rafe.

She'd never love again. She'd resigned herself to spinsterhood. She'd find her calling, make it on her own. And live out her days alone. She found herself smiling. Maybe she'd live out her days with her widowed mother.

The widowed mother she'd decided to forgive.

She'd wasted too much of her precious life being petty. Life was too short to hold grudges. Love was too precious to let slip away. And she did love her mother. She might have been Daddy's girl, but she'd always adored her Mama.

"Fine. Go ahead."

"I'm getting a divorce."

"Not on my account, I hope."

"On my own account. I married for the wrong reasons, like you said."

She widened her eyes. Was his marriage truly over? Did she dare hope? "What do you mean?"

She listened as he told her about the woman named Lilia who lived with his father. Who'd fallen in love with his father.

"But we figured it out. Dallas McCray talked to an immigration attorney in Denver, and I can get my divorce. I would have gotten it anyway, but the attorney fixed it so Lilia doesn't have to go back to Mexico. She can stay here and keep her green card."

"That's nice, Rafe. I'm happy for her. And for you."

"I'm sorry I couldn't help you save your ranch. The divorce won't be final for six months."

"No worries. There are more important things in life than the ranch."

Strange words, coming from Angie Bay. But she meant every one. There were so many more important things. Like love. She regarded the beautiful bronze man who'd captured her heart. Could he have ever loved her?

"Yes, there are more important things than the ranch," he agreed. "Like people."

She nodded. Thirty-two was a late age to learn that valuable lesson, but at least she'd learned it.

"Would you marry for love, Angie?"

"Yes, of course I would."

"Would you... Would you marry me?"

She widened her eyes. "What?"

"I love you, Angelina." He dropped down to one knee. "Would you be my wife?"

She dropped down next to him. His words echoed in her mind, their sound sweeter than a Mozart sonata, sweeter than a baby's laugh. "Say it again?"

He took both her hands in his. "I love you more than life itself. I swear I'll take care of you. It might be a modest life, but

I'll work two jobs if I have to. I'll kick Tom out of the apartment and you can move in. Or we'll find our own place. A better place. I'll do anything, if only you'll say yes. Please, Angie. I love you."

Tears welled in her eyes. He loved her.

And suddenly nothing else mattered. Not the ranch she'd lost, not the fact that he'd already been married, not that her mother had lied to her entire life, and even not that the father she'd adored had been her uncle, not her biological father. Nothing mattered but Rafe and their love for each other.

His gaze penetrated her. "Do you... Do you think you could grow to love me?"

She threw her arms around his neck. "Rafe, I already do. I've loved you for so long."

He clenched her in a bear hug. "I'll bust my ass to provide for you, I swear it."

"Oh, Rafe, Rafe. I love you so much."

"I promise I'll take care of you. I'll treasure you. You're my most precious thing in the world."

She whimpered silently into his shoulder.

"I'm sorry I couldn't save your ranch for you. I'll find some way to make it up to you. I promise, baby. I'll give you a good life."

She sniffed and choked back a sob. "I don't care about the ranch anymore. All I need is you and our love."

Her phone vibrated in her pocket. "I'm sorry, I have to take this. My mother told me if she called today to take the call. That it'd be important."

"I understand," Rafe said. "Go ahead."

"Yeah, Mama?" she said into the phone.

"Angie, you need to come over to the house right away. It's important."

"All right. We'll be right there."

"We?"

"I'll explain when I get there. I love you. Goodbye." She clicked the phone off and turned back to Rafe. "I need to go to my mother's, and I want you to come with me."

"Okay, but why?"

"My mama says it's important, and I want you with me to hear anything important. You're my fiancé now, and everything that involves me involves you."

He smiled. "I kind of like that."

"I kind of do too."

When they reached the house, Angie and Rafe walked in hand in hand.

Her mother greeted her with tears in her eyes. Jefferson Bay sat on the sofa in the living room.

"Oh, Angie," Maria said, "did you mean it?"

"Mean what?"

"When you said you loved me. Did you mean it?"

She smiled, love warming her heart. "I did, Mama. I'm forgiving you. I will always love Daddy, and he was my real daddy in every way that mattered. You did what you felt you had to do at the time. It will take some time for me to deal with it, but I love you."

"Angie, what's this about?" Rafe asked.

"Oh, I'm sorry. Mama, this is Rafe Grayhawk."

"Yes, hello, Rafe. We've met. How are you?"

"I'm fine, ma'am."

"Rafe is here because...well, because he's the man I love. We're getting married."

"Angie! That's wonderful! But you don't have to now. I've—"

"I'm not getting married because I have to. I'm getting married because I want to. Rafe and I are in love. But we can't be married for at least six months."

"Why not?"

Rafe stepped forward. "Because of me, ma'am. I'm real sorry I couldn't save Angie's ranch. To make a long story short, I made a decision five years ago and didn't consider all the consequences. I married someone else to help her out of a bind. It was never a real marriage. I've got an attorney and we're dissolving the marriage. But it won't happen in time to save the ranch. I'm very sorry."

Maria Bay touched his forearm. "Do you love my daughter?"

"With all my heart, ma'am."

"And Angie, you love him?"

"Mama, I love him something awful. I can't imagine my life without him."

She smiled and wiped her eyes. "Then I'm so very happy for both of you. And I have more wonderful news. Tell them, Jeff."

Jefferson Bay stood. "I have decided not to take the inheritance away from you. Since you are my rightful heir anyway, even if I did, it would go to you eventually. So I want you to have it now." He handed her an envelope. "Here's a document signing over my interest in the ranch to you. Your brother drafted it. It's all legal."

"Jeff is staying here at Cha Cha with me," Maria said. "We've decided to put the past behind us and try to recapture our friendship."

"Mama, you don't have to do this for me."

"She's not," Jeff said. "It was my idea. I thought long and

hard and decided I didn't want to live out the rest of my life as a bitter old man. I know you don't think of me as your father. Maybe you never will. I understand if that's the case and I will respect your wishes. I would love to cultivate a relationship with you, but I'm willing to do it on your terms. And if you're not interested, I will accept that."

"I don't know what to say," Angie said. "Thank you, I guess."

"Please don't thank me. I'm ashamed of the way I've acted. Even if you weren't my daughter, I'm not sure I could have gone through with it. I always envied Wayne. It's time to put those bad feelings to rest."

He stepped forward and held his hand out to Rafe. "I'm Jefferson Bay, Angie's uncle...and biological father."

Rafe's eyes widened. "Oh?"

Angie wrapped her arms around him. "It's a long story, Rafe. I'll tell you all about it tonight, okay?"

"Okay, baby."

"What do you do, Rafe?" Jeff asked.

"I'm a ranch hand for Chad McCray, Angie's brother-in-law. I also give riding lessons." He winked at Angie.

"Then I'm sure you'll be a huge help to Angie at Bay Crossing," Jeff said. "You all can move out there anytime and get settled."

"Well, half of it belongs to Catie," Angie said.

"Catie's content at McCray Landing with Chad," Maria said. "She trusts you to see to her interests. The ranch is yours to run, Angelina."

She smiled up at her handsome fiancé. "*Ours* to run."

EPILOGUE

A cool spring breeze drifted over Angie as she stood in the receiving line after her modest wedding at Bay Crossing. Beside her stood her husband, tall and proud, his onyx locks tied behind his neck in a black strip of leather. Black dress pants and a white button-down open at the collar accentuated his ruggedly handsome looks. Angie wore a casual white sheath cut to mid-knee. Her dark hair fell in waves brushing her shoulders.

Nearly eight months had passed since her biological father had given her his share of the ranch, and Rafe's divorce from Lilia had been final a month ago.

Beside the groom stood his brother, also dressed casually, his wavy black hair brushing his collar, looking nearly as handsome as Rafe himself. Next to Angie was Catie, her belly swollen with the next McCray heir who was due to make an appearance any day.

Next to Tom, Lilia shone in a pastel blue dress, the golden band shining on her left ring finger. Jack Grayhawk beamed next to his new wife. On Catie's other side, Maria radiated happiness in her peacock-blue day dress, and Jefferson Bay was as handsome as his older brother in brown slacks and a tan shirt. Their relationship was still tenuous, but it was mending. They could smile and laugh together now, and Jeff no longer seemed so angry. It would take time, but Angie hoped they'd both find love again. Her mother—and her father—deserved happiness. She sincerely hoped they'd find what she'd found with Rafe. Would it be with each other? She didn't know yet, but the possibility existed.

"Congratulations, you two." Annie McCray gave Angie a loose hug so as not to squish the baby boy she held in her arms. Her husband, Dallas, held the other, while their twin girls, Sylvie and Laurie, toddled between their parents.

"Which one is this?" Angie asked.

"This is Jason, and Dallas has Jon."

"Twins again," Rafe said, smiling. "And this time boys."

"Lord, yes," Annie said. "Two sets of twins are more than enough." She curved her lips upward in a sly smile. "I made a little appointment for Dallas at the doctor's office next week."

Rafe and Angie laughed.

"Not too funny from where I'm standin'," Dallas said.

"You'll be fine," Rafe said, chuckling. "Just stock up on frozen peas. I've heard they work like a charm."

Dallas swatted him on the arm. "I'll be interested to see how jovial you are about it when it's your turn."

"It won't be your turn for a while," Angie said, after Dallas had moved on. "I want a slew of little Grayhawks running around here."

Rafe smiled. So handsome. She'd never tire of looking at her magnificent husband.

"I don't have a problem with that. Not at all. In fact, we'll practice tonight."

She lifted her chin, and he met her mouth with his own. A quick peck. After all, they had a ton more people to greet.

"I can't wait."

CONTINUE THE TEMPTATION SAGA WITH BOOK FIVE

Treasuring

AMBER

Available Now

Keep reading for an excerpt!

CHAPTER ONE

"You want me to come to a baby shower? Are you kiddin' me?" Harper Bay paced the length of his father's—now *his*—office in his mother's—now *his*—ranch house.

His little sister's sigh cut right through the phone. "Couples showers are the new thing now, Harp. Amber says—"

"Sheesh, Catie." Harper Bay rolled his eyes, thankful his sister couldn't see him through the phone. He was damn sick of hearing what Amber Cross had to say. That bleached blond manicurist who had become Catie's new soul sister spouted off all kinds of newfangled ideas, and he didn't like a one of them. "Dallas and Annie just had the twins a month ago, and none of us guys had to go to a shower. And you forget one important little detail."

"What's that?"

"Last time I checked, I'm not a 'couple.'"

"Co-ed shower, then. We're talking semantics here." Catie's tone softened. "Don't you want to welcome little Violet?"

How in hell does she do that? Her petal-soft voice never failed to make him wilt. He was a sucker for his baby sister, and he'd be just as much of a sucker for his new niece. Violet was a beauty even at a week old, with a mop of black hair and eyes the darkest sapphire blue. They'd probably turn big and brown like Catie's. She'd be a heartbreaker for sure.

But a baby shower? He was a man, for God's sake. A

damned cowboy. Cowboys did not go to baby showers. That had to be in a rulebook somewhere.

He shook his head. "What's Chad think of this nonsense?"

"Chad says 'whatever makes me happy.'"

Christ.

Whipped.

Harper had known Chad McCray most of his life. A bigger womanizer hadn't existed on the planet...until Catie reeled him in. Now Chad was the epitome of whipped. His face was probably next to "whipped" in the damned dictionary. Harper couldn't prevent a chuckle.

"What are you laughing at?" Catie demanded.

Why not be honest? "Just your whipped hubby, that's all."

"For your information, Chad is *not* whipped."

"Give me a break, Catie-bug. You have the cowboy wrapped around your little finger, and it won't be long till that pretty little daughter of yours has him twisted around hers, too."

Catie's soft laugh gave her away. She knew her husband was whipped. Heck, she was whipped, too. Those two were crazy about each other. Crazy in a way his and Catie's parents had never been. Crazy in a way Harper had never been and probably never would be. He had a ranch to run now. When his father passed away several months ago, Harper had become sole owner of Cha Cha Ranch outside of Bakersville, Colorado. His mother, who'd inherited the ranch when Harper was a boy and transferred it to her husband, still lived in the big ranch house and would for as long as she wished. His uncle, Jefferson Bay, also lived there. Jeff had been estranged from the family for the last three decades, and they were slowly— very slowly—rebuilding their relationship.

Nope, no "whipped" for Harper. He had too much to do. Too many responsibilities. He wasn't sure when he'd last had a date.

How long had it been since he'd had sex?

Too damn long. Had they changed it?

"Harp?"

Reality. Catie. Sometimes the magnitude of owning a whole beef ranch overwhelmed him. "Sorry, just thinking." He sat down in his father's—*his*—chair. "I really think I'll pass on the shower thing, Sis."

"Please? Rafe is coming with Angie. They're coming in from the western slope just to attend."

"They haven't seen Violet yet. They're coming to see her, not for the shower."

"So they'll kill two birds with one stone."

"I suppose they will. I, however, have already seen my beautiful niece, and I plan to see her a lot. Just not during some girly shower."

"It's not going to be a girly shower."

"Oh yeah? You getting a stripper?"

Another sigh from Catie. "Geez, Harp."

"Sorry." Though he wouldn't mind seeing Amber Cross strut her stuff naked. Damn, she had the body of a stripper. Lithe long legs curled around a silver pole, platinum locks falling over rosy-skinned shoulders...pink nipples peeking through...

His groin tightened.

Christ. His body betrayed him. Amber was so not his type. Though she was a Texas native and the reigning Bakersville Rodeo Queen, she was about as far from the girls Harper had grown up with as Maine was from California. Cute Colorado farm girl? *Hell, no.* Nearly white tresses, long red fingernails, leather miniskirts, and sequined tube tops...

Damn, the woman was hot.

Hot, and a major pain in the ass with her couples shower. She'd had Catie doing all kinds of weird crap in the last year. Thursday night happy hour at The Bullfrog had become a tradition for his baby sister. She never missed it, even when she'd been big as a house with Violet. Virgin drinks, yes, but still out on the dance floor shakin' her booty with her new BFF.

He couldn't believe Chad allowed it. Heck, of course he did. The man was so whipped.

"So are you coming or not?"

"You know I love you and I love Violet." He sighed. "But no. I'm sorry."

"Have it your way, then. Everybody else in town will be here."

"Tell everybody else I said hi."

"Fine." Her voice cracked. "Goodbye." Catie's phone clicked.

He didn't want to hurt her, but a baby shower? Sorry, this cowboy wasn't turning in his man card.

★ ★ ★

"Hey, Tom, give me a Fat Tire."

"Comin' up." Tom Grayhawk, the bartender, smiled. "What's eatin' at you tonight?"

"Nothin'." Harper turned and looked toward the door. "Oh crap."

"Now what?"

"Here comes that damn Amber."

Tom chuckled. "Damn Amber? She's a luscious thing in my book."

"Hot as hell," Harper agreed, "but not my type."

"Hot as hell isn't your type?" Tom slid a bottle of beer across the wooden counter.

"This particular girl is definitely not my type. Do you know she wants me to—"

"Harper Bay."

Amber's voice was low and sultry, like the smoky aroma of aged bourbon. She slid onto the bar stool next to Harper and crossed her long tan legs. The woman was always a light bronze, even now, in springtime. Had to be fake. Her denim miniskirt hardly covered her thighs as she sat. Harper tried not to stare.

"What'll it be, beautiful?" Tom asked.

"Like you have to ask?" Her long brown eyelashes batted at Tom.

Harper's jeans seemed tight. He wiggled uneasily on his stool.

"One cosmo comin' up," Tom said.

"So," Amber said.

Harper cleared his throat. "So what?"

"You've got your little sister in a dither over this shower thing. She can't stand the thought of you not being there."

He let out a huff. "She'll get used to it. Men don't belong at baby showers. Why didn't she have the shower months ago, anyway? Before Violet was born?"

"'Cause she and Chad didn't want to know the sex. They wanted to be surprised in the delivery room. So I advised—"

"You advised? Another one of your cockamamie ideas?"

She shook her head and rolled her eyes. Totally blowing

him off. Why did that irk him so much?

"I advised her to wait till the baby was born so people could bring gender appropriate gifts. It made perfect sense to Catie. Who wants a bunch of yellow and green baby clothes?"

"Yellow and green?"

"Yes, yellow and green. No one buys blue or pink when they don't know the sex. Everyone knows that."

He smirked. "Pardon me. I missed the lecture on baby shower purchasing etiquette."

Amber pursed her lips. "Was that supposed to be funny?"

"Hardly. None of this is funny from where I'm standin'. I am not going to a baby shower. Case closed."

Tom set the cosmo in front of Amber. "Simmer down, Harp. I'm going. It'll be a great party."

"Am I truly the only guy left in this town who thinks this is an atrocity?"

"I didn't say that, but the baby is your niece. She's my brother's niece. So I'm going to pay my respects. Besides, Chad McCray throws a great party."

"See?" Amber said. "Tom knows what he's talking about. You've really upset Catie. Besides, couples showers aren't anything new. They're all the rage in Texas."

"Well, we certainly want to do everything the way they do in Texas." Harper shook his head. "But last time I checked, I'm not a couple."

"Neither am I," Tom said, "but I'm going. I'm tagging along with my dad and Lilia."

"I'm not a couple either," Amber said. "So what?"

Tom curved his lips upward in a lopsided smile.

Shit. He's up to no good.

"Why don't you two go together?"

Good God in heaven.

Amber would say something, surely. She'd shoot that idea down. The two of them had less in common than Jesus and the devil. Harper waited, tense.

Come on, Amber. Speak. Tell him you'd rather be hung out by your toenails than be my date at some couples shower.

"I'm free if you are," she said coyly.

Christ.

"Well, then, you all have a date." Tom smiled and raised one eyebrow.

Damn it, Grayhawk, I owe you one. "I can't be her date since I'm not going."

There. Still a save.

"No, no, no," Tom said. "This lovely lady needs an escort. And you don't want to disappoint your pretty little sister."

Hitting him right where it hurt. And now he had to take Amber to the party on top of everything else. Either that or reject her right here. Even though they had no interest in each other, he was too much of a gentleman to do that.

He gritted his teeth. "Fine."

Amber winked at Tom and sipped her cosmo. "Perfect. I'll look forward to seeing you. Pick me up at the beauty shop on Saturday at two."

Tom winked back.

Harper downed the last of his beer and plunked the bottle on the bar. *Damn it all.*

He'd just been played like a fiddle.

MESSAGE FROM HELEN HARDT

Dear Reader,

Thank you for reading *Taming Angelina*. If you want to find out about my current backlist and future releases, please like my Facebook page: **www.facebook.com/HelenHardt** and join my mailing list: **www.helenhardt.com/signup/**. I often do giveaways. If you're a fan and would like to join my street team to help spread the word about my books, you can do so here: **www.facebook.com/groups/hardtandsoul/**. I regularly do awesome giveaways for my street team members.

If you enjoyed the story, please take the time to leave a review on a site like Amazon or Goodreads. I welcome all feedback.

I wish you all the best!

Helen

ALSO BY HELEN HARDT

The Sex and the Season Series:
Lily and the Duke
Rose in Bloom
Lady Alexandra's Lover
Sophie's Voice
The Perils of Patricia (Coming Soon)

The Temptation Saga:
Tempting Dusty
Teasing Annie
Taking Catie
Taming Angelina
Treasuring Amber
Trusting Sydney
Tantalizing Maria

The Steel Brothers Saga:
Craving
Obsession
Possession
Melt (Coming December 20th, 2016)
Burn (Coming February 14th, 2017)
Surrender (Coming May 16th, 2017)

Daughters of the Prairie:
The Outlaw's Angel
Lessons of the Heart
Song of the Raven

ACKNOWLEDGMENTS

Taming Angelina sees Angie go from a spoiled brat to a strong woman who realizes what is truly important in life. I hope you enjoyed the story of her and Rafe.

So many people helped along the way in bringing this book to you. Celina Summers, Michele Hamner Moore, Jenny Rarden, Coreen Montagna, Kelly Shorten, David Grishman, Meredith Wild, Jonathan Mac, Kurt Vachon, Yvonne Ellis, Shayla Fereshetian—thank you all for your expertise and guidance. Eternal thanks to Waterhouse Press for the expert rebranding of the series.

And thanks most of all to you, the readers. Up next, Angie and Catie's brother, Harper, finally gets a story of his own, and his heroine? None other than the striking Texan, Amber Cross. Enjoy their story, *Treasuring Amber*.

ABOUT THE AUTHOR

New York Times and *USA Today* Bestselling author Helen Hardt's passion for the written word began with the books her mother read to her at bedtime. She wrote her first story at age six and hasn't stopped since. In addition to being an award winning author of contemporary and historical romance and erotica, she's a mother, a black belt in Taekwondo, a grammar geek, an appreciator of fine red wine, and a lover of Ben and Jerry's ice cream. She writes from her home in Colorado, where she lives with her family. Helen loves to hear from readers.

Visit her here:
www.facebook.com/HelenHardt

AVAILABLE NOW FROM
HELEN HARDT

After being left at the altar, Jade Roberts seeks solace at her best friend's ranch on the Colorado western slope. Her humiliation still ripe, she doesn't expect to be attracted to her friend's reticent brother, but when the gorgeous cowboy kisses her, all bets are off.

Talon Steel is broken. Having never fully healed from a horrific childhood trauma, he simply exists, taking from women what is offered and giving nothing in return...until Jade Roberts catapults into his life. She is beautiful, sweet, and giving, and his desire for her becomes a craving he fears he'll never be able to satisfy.

Passion sizzles between the two lovers...but long-buried secrets haunt them both and may eventually tear them apart.

Visit HelenHardt.com for more information!

ALSO AVAILABLE FROM
HELEN HARDT

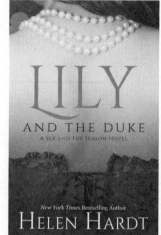

Lady Lily Jameson is thrilled to attend a house party given by Daniel Farnsworth, the Duke of Lybrook, but not because he's the most eligible bachelor in the peerage. Her only interest is his famous art collection, which reputedly includes a painting by her favorite artist, Jan Vermeer.

Daniel, duke only by virtue of the untimely deaths of his father and older brother, wants nothing to do with his new duties. He'd rather continue his rakish ways. When he finds the lovely Lily sneaking around the property in search of his art collection, sparks fly.

Despite her father's wishes, Lily has no intention of marrying. She wants to travel the world to gain real life inspiration for her painting and writing. And what could be better worldly experience than a passionate affair with the notorious Duke of Lybrook?

But circumstances may change the game and the players...and danger lurks, as well.

Visit HelenHardt.com for more information!

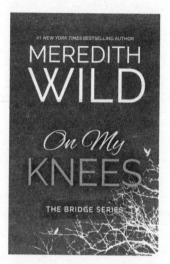